T0154426

Outside the Flock

by

JACKIE CALHOUN

Ferndale, Michigan
2003

Bella Books, Inc.
P.O. Box 201007
Ferndale, MI 48220

Printed in the United States of America on acid-free paper
First Edition

Photo of Jackie Calhoun by Paul Siket
Cover designer: Bonnie Liss (Phoenix Graphics)

ISBN 1-931513-13-9

Dedicated to my sisters,
Chris Calhoun and Kay Bird

Acknowledgments

With thanks to the following:

Joan Hendry, my first reader

Diane Mandler for her support

Kelly Smith and Terese Orban and the people at Bella Books

My friends and family

Prologue

Staring out the passenger window, Jo repeated silently the words she had memorized to tell Mark she was leaving. She barely noticed the office buildings set back on green lawns or the speeding traffic flowing around their Lincoln, as if it were an obstacle, until a blaring horn startled her.

"Hey," Mark said, alarmed.

Her head snapped forward as a Mercedes drifted from the inside lane into theirs, so close it seemed the German sedan would skim their front bumper if Mark didn't move out of the way. She opened her mouth to yell a warning, but Mark was already braking and swerving into the outside lane.

A jolt from the rear took her by surprise as a pickup truck shoved their Lincoln into the Mercedes. What she remembered later was the noise: horns blowing, brakes screeching, metal tearing, Mark yelling "fuck, fuck, fuck," someone screaming. The Lincoln climbed over the Mercedes as the pickup tore into their car, pushing her against the air bag.

The pain in her ribcage caused her to gasp, to realize that she was the one screaming. Taking a breath became suddenly excruciating, and she shut up.

All momentum jarred to a stop when the Lincoln came to a halt atop the Mercedes with the hood of the pickup in its backseat. Flashing blue and red lights circled the tangled vehicles. Her ears rang. The front doors of the Lincoln Continental had popped opened under pressure, and they twisted and creaked. Had they not been belted in she would have been thrown onto that spreading smear of oil. She wondered which car it belonged to. It didn't matter. All three vehicles were surely totaled.

"Are you all right, Jo?" Mark asked. The air bag had popped out of the steering wheel and pinned him to the back of the seat.

Hers had jumped out of the dash. It was hard to breathe and hurt to talk. "I guess. Are you?"

"I can't move, but I don't feel any pain. They'll get us out of here."

A medical attendant squatted in the open door and told her not to move till they could put a neck brace on her. "We have to pull the pickup out of the way before we can get you out. Can you hang in there?" he asked.

As if she could move, she thought, her voice sounding small and strange when she said, "Yes."

"Good girl." He touched her shoulder and left.

"Mark?" Pinned in place as she was, she could only see the shattered windshield in front of her and whatever was in her peripheral vision. "Are they putting a neck brace on you too?"

"It's only a precaution," he said.

Her neck immediately began to hurt.

The problem became separating the vehicles. Whenever the tow truck pulled the pickup backwards, the Lincoln moved with it. She ground her teeth as metal grated on metal. Each jerk on the pickup resulted in a corresponding yank of the Lincoln that made her gasp anew.

Her back and neck ached. The nerves in her legs had begun to jump. Then someone gave her a shot.

I

The blood pressure cuff tightened on her arm, wakening her to a room so white that she squinted at the walls and sheets as if they were fresh snow in sunlight. The collar wrapped around her neck held her head rigidly in place.

"Hi." The nurse standing by her bed smiled. "How do you feel?"

She risked a deep breath. A mistake. The pain was immediate, making her gasp. "Rotten. Why the neck piece?"

"Whiplash. You were hit from behind. The good news is nothing is broken. Except for a couple cracked ribs you're in one piece."

She remembered being scanned as if it had been a dream. "Where's Mark? He came in with me."

"Across the hall."

"Is he all right?"

"Ask him yourself. You can phone his room." The woman picked up the receiver, punched in a number, and handed it over.

"It's me. Are you okay?" she asked.

"I was in your room, but I didn't want to wake you up. How do you feel?"

"Why are you in the hospital if you're all right?"

"There was some blood in my urine. We were lucky, hon. Want some company?"

She didn't feel lucky. She felt fragile. "I'm not much fun right now."

In less than a minute he was there — all six foot, one hundred ninety pounds — lowering himself carefully into a chair next to the bed. He, too, wore a neck brace. The skin surrounding his eyes was bruised.

"You don't look so hot," she said.

"The air bag."

"I thought air bags were supposed to save you, not hurt you."

"They are." He grimaced as he shifted in the chair. "I never saw that pickup. I must have pulled right in front of it." His vivid blue eyes met hers. "What was it you wanted to talk about before all that happened?"

"I can't remember."

"I'm not surprised."

She hadn't forgotten. She'd lost courage. Had he no clue? "Did you call anyone?"

"Ted. He'll come to get us and take us home." She'd first met Mark's son from his former marriage when he was sixteen. A polite boy, he was a kind man at thirty.

"Good," she said. "When will that be?"

"For me, tomorrow. We'll have to see about you."

"I'm all right. What's a cracked rib or two? That's all it is, right?"

"Yeah, but it's not up to me."

The thought that it could have been much worse, that she could have died released chills. "I should call Kimberly. She can phone work for me tomorrow morning." Her sister must wonder why they weren't home. There were probably ten messages on the answering machine from Kimberly.

"And I better go call John." Mark's partner in his law office.

Again alone, she picked up the receiver and punched in Gail's work number. "Hi, it's me," she whispered, comforted by the familiar voice, warm and a little husky. How had one person assumed such importance that her voice alone could soothe?

"Where are you?" Gail asked.

"In the hospital. I'll call you when I get out. Probably tomorrow." She spoke quickly, afraid that Mark might reappear.

"What happened?" Gail asked, her voice alarmed.

"An accident. I'm okay. I have to go, though. I love you." She'd told Gail she'd tell Mark over the weekend. She hadn't. How could she tell him she couldn't live with him anymore without telling him why?

The ringing phone pulled her out of a dream. Fumbling for the receiver, she dropped it against the side rails before bringing it to her ear.

"What the hell happened?" Her sister demanded.

"How did you find out?" Kimberly always knew what she was up to. A year apart, they'd grown up attuned to one another. They'd both even married attorneys. How would Kimberly react to her leaving Mark for Gail?

"John told Brad." Mark's partner had passed on the news to Kimberly's husband.

"I was going to call you. I fell asleep," she said. "Did John tell Brad how it happened?"

"I want to hear it from you."

"Phone the office for me tomorrow, will you? Tell Walter I won't be in." She related the details of the accident as best she could remember. Rarely did Kimberly listen to her without interruption. Her sister was quiet. If Jo hadn't heard some of her kids in the background, she'd have asked if she was still there.

"God, you could be dead," Kim said with horror, when Jo finished. "What would I do without you?"

It was then she decided to confide in her. "Kim, I have to talk to you. Not on the phone, though."

"I'll come over when you get home. If I'd known, I'd have gone to the hospital today."

"Never mind that. It's too far. Let's have lunch during the week. My place. Okay?"

"There's something else? I knew it," Kimberly said.

"This will surprise you, I promise," she added.

"I doubt it."

It did, though. Kimberly stared at Jo over the kitchen table. Her mouth opened without sound. She recovered quickly. "Remember that married guy you fell in love with before Mark? You were crazy about him."

It didn't make sense to Jo either. "Yes, but do you recall my best friend in high school, Dorothy Adams? I was crazy about her too. And Margie Langston, and Lisa Olski."

"I guess I knew deep down inside." Kimberly sighed, her hand on her chest. "Have you told Mark?"

Jo shook her head. "I don't know how to tell him. This accident woke me up, though. It's now or never. I'm in my forties."

"And Gail? Are you going to live with her?"

"That's what she wants."

"Does she have kids?"

"A girl." Connie was that awful age when puberty begins to take hold in girls — thirteen. She was sullen, snotty, and smart-mouthed.

"Don't tell Mother, okay?" Their mother lived in Florida with her second husband. Kimberly and Jo's father had left when she and her sister were too young to remember.

"You'll have to tell her sometime," Kimberly said.

"I'll just be living up to her expectations. Maybe she'll be pleased." She dreaded the long pause she knew would follow the telling, the swift disapproval that would ensue.

"She loves us as much as she loves anybody," Kimberly said with a grim laugh.

"Does she? I've always wondered."

Kimberly glanced at the clock and stood up. "I've got to go. Max is playing Little League this afternoon."

"How should I tell Mark?" Jo stepped away from her sister's hug. It hurt to sit, to stand, to breathe, to lie down.

"Maybe you better wait till your ribs heal."

She walked outdoors with Kim and turned her face to the hot sunshine. She'd lie in the chaise longue by the pool after Kimberly left. Maybe the warm rays would reach inside and mend her broken parts.

Kimberly slid behind the wheel of her Audi station wagon. "I don't envy you. Are you going to tell Mark about Gail?"

"No."

"And if he asks why you're moving in with her?" She was squinting up at Jo.

"She's a friend. Do I have to tell?" she asked.

"Sooner or later, he'll guess."

"Then he'll realize he's not being rejected for another man, won't he?"

Kimberly reached through the open window and squeezed her hand. "I wish it were different, Jo. I like Mark."

"I love him." Her voice broke a little.

"Not enough." Kimberly sighed and tucked a hank of hair behind one small ear.

"Not the right way. Don't ask why I married him. Denial is a way of life."

Kimberly waved an arm through the open window as the Audi carried her away.

II

"Hey, wake up." Cool fingertips brushed her forehead.

"Hi," she said hoarsely, a surge of excitement working its way through her. Gail stood between her and the sun. Her chin length, wavy hair was lit from behind. "You look like an angel."

"I'm anything but as you well know." Gail's bell-like laugh made Jo smile. "I had to see for myself that you were all right."

She pushed herself up a little, wincing at the pain, and touched the collar she still wore. "Sit down, so I can see you better. I can't turn my head."

Perching on the chaise longue next to hers, Gail said, "Aren't you going to miss all this?"

"What?" She knew Gail meant the pool, the expensive cars, the lavish house, the ability to buy things without having to choose. Should she get the blouse or go out for dinner? That was the kind of choice she didn't have to make now.

"I suppose you'll receive a good settlement."

She followed Gail's gaze to the pool, blue and inviting. She hadn't gotten past how she was going to tell Mark that she wanted out after sixteen years of marriage. "I haven't thought that far ahead."

"When are you coming over?" Gail asked.

"Friday."

"Connie will be at her dad's, if she doesn't change her mind. God, she's difficult right now."

"It won't get easier if I'm around," she said.

Gail blinked long lashes. "I know. We aren't at that point yet, are we? Did you tell Mark?"

"I will," she promised, feeling anxious. "How did you tell Conrad?" Gail's ex-husband.

"He made it easy. He told me he had someone else." Gail's mouth twisted.

"You never said. How did it feel?"

"Rejection never feels good, even if you want out." Gail stood up and smiled down at her. Bending over, she kissed Jo on the forehead. "I'll see you Friday. Don't get up."

She struggled to her feet anyway, and they walked around the house to the circular driveway. She felt momentarily bereft when Gail drove away.

Glancing at her watch, she went inside to the bathroom, Stripping off her clothes, she turned on the water and let the tub fill at her feet. Normally, she would shower, but she shrank at the thought of water bouncing off her ribcage. Turning on the whirlpool spouts, she lowered herself into the hot depths.

Mark found her there.

"Thanks," she said, taking one of the drinks he carried. It tasted wonderfully cool. "How was work?"

He loosened his tie. "Crazy. Want to sue the Mercedes people who cut us off? John thinks we should."

"Then whoever was in the pickup could sue us."

He laughed. "You're pretty sharp. Which makes me wonder if you should be drinking when you're on pain meds."

"I won't take any meds tonight," she promised.

He helped her out of the tub and began drying her with a towel. When she cringed at his touch, he turned the hair dryer on her wet body.

She laughed and then began to cry.

"I didn't mean to hurt you." He turned off the dryer, his face concerned.

"It's not that."

"What is it then?"

"I like you. In fact, I love you." Her voice broke.

"The feeling's mutual." His frown turned into a big grin.

"And I have to leave you. I'm so sorry."

He stood with sleeves rolled up, the towel dangling from one large hand, gazing at her with puzzled eyes. "What?"

"I want to be on my own. I need to be on my own." She searched for some reason other than the real one for separating, something that would make sense.

"Why?" he asked. "Is there someone else?"

"Yes." Gently, she took the towel and wrapped it around herself.

He followed her out of the bathroom to where they slept, a large sunny room that overlooked the pool. Her heart contracted at the thought of Mark lying alone in the king-size bed.

"Do you want a child? We can still have one."

She'd given that idea up when she turned forty. Kimberly had more than enough babies for both of them. "No."

"What can someone else give you that I can't?"

She turned, the towel tucked tightly under her arms. "I'm a lesbian, Mark." In the full length mirror near the door her skin glowed a fiery red against the white terry cloth. She was ashamed.

He looked amazed. "Was it all an act? Our marriage?"

"No. I do love you. It's not you. It's me."

"I don't want you to go." He sat on the bed, his shoulders slumped. "If you love me, why leave?"

"I need a woman." Gail. She sat down next to him, and his fingers closed tightly around hers.

"You can have one, if you're discreet," he said in a soft voice. She wondered if she'd heard right. "Is that where you go on Fridays? To see a woman?"

"Yes," she admitted.

He looked at her, his blue eyes flat. "It was the accident, wasn't it?"

She nodded. "I might have died." The rest of it stuck in her craw. She couldn't say without ever finding out what it was like to live with a woman, with Gail. "But I was trying to tell you before the accident happened," she added.

Sarcasm edged into his voice. "How long have you known this?"

She knew exactly. When she met Gail at the Y. "I finally admitted it to myself a year ago."

His face darkened. "And I thought this marriage was for good."

She asked, "Why are you home early?"

He replied gloomily, "I wanted to see how you were feeling."

She felt rotten. "I'm going back to work tomorrow."

Getting off the bed, he changed into shorts and a T-shirt. His body had altered little over the years, showing only the bare beginnings of a paunch. His dark hair, although streaked with gray, was still thick and resistant to control.

With difficulty, she pulled a clean T-shirt over her head and stepped into shorts herself. For sixteen years they'd taken off their clothes in front of each other without embarrassment. How could it feel awkward now?

"I'll fix dinner," he said.

She stretched out carefully on the bed. The windows were open, and sunshine flowed in on a soft, warm breeze. Listening to the birds, she tried to identify them by their songs.

Mark brought her awake with a touch on the shoulder. He set a dinner tray with soup, a grilled cheese sandwich, a salad, a bottle of wine and two glasses on the comforter.

"Did you eat?" she asked.

"While I cooked," he said.

She tried to spoon the canned soup but ended up picking up the bowl and slurping it down.

Refilling his wine glass, he said stiffly, "Please don't tell anyone else."

She promised, hoping Kimberly hadn't told Brad. She'd give her a call later.

Waking in the semi-dark room, she rolled onto her side and put her feet on the floor. She heard Mark's measured breathing. Getting to her feet, she pulled on her terry cloth robe, then quietly left the room. Street lights provided enough illumination for her to walk through the house without turning on lights.

She placed the call from the den and thought of how the ringing would resonate through the rooms in Gail's small house.

The receiver banged against something before Gail muttered, "Hello."

"It's me," she whispered.

"Ah, me," Gail said, her tone softening. "What does me want?"

"Just to hear your voice."

"Is that what you called to tell me at three in the morning?"

"I told Mark."

Silence. "And?"

"He doesn't want me to leave, but he won't stop me from seeing you." She knew she was saying it all wrong.

Gail's voice became clearer, louder. "Let me ask you this. Would you let him stop you from seeing me?"

"No, but he would rather have me see you than have me leave." She didn't know how Gail would react to this. Connie was a wild card. It might be better all the way around if she didn't move in.

"I think you want to have your cake and eat it, too."

"Can we talk about this Friday?"

"I'm not the one who called at three in the morning," Gail snapped.

In the silence that followed Jo heard an almost inaudible click. Either Mark or Connie had hung up. "We have an eavesdropper. Good night."

She dozed in the chair until the birds woke her. Walking stiffly out through the sunporch to the pool, she ran out of steam and lowered herself onto one of the straighter chairs. She breathed shallowly of the cool, early morning air.

Shades of red and yellow stained the eastern horizon. The moon dangled low in a pale blue sky. Dew glistened on the grass and delicate spider webs hung between bushes. Such a morning gave hope that everything could work out. Fat chance, she thought.

She looked up as Mark handed her a cup of coffee. "Thanks. You're up early."

"It was lonely in bed." He stretched out on a chaise

lounge, hairy legs and arms protruding from his robe. "Couldn't you sleep?"

She said, "I don't think what you suggested is such a good idea."

"If it doesn't work out, you can leave."

He hadn't thought this through. She let it go.

III

With a grunt, she set down her suitcase in Gail's tiny front hall and laid her work clothes on hangers over it. She had enough clothes to get her through Monday. She'd packed after the front door closed behind Mark, then left a note on the fridge. Next week she'd go back when he was gone and get more. Maybe Kimberly would help.

"Hey, babe," she said softly as Gail came toward her. "Are you alone?" Connie might be lurking around the corner. The girl pretended Jo didn't exist. When Jo talked to her, she often replied through her mother.

Gail's arms closed around her without pressure. She stiffened, expecting pain. They were the same height, but Jo thought Gail, who was younger, was softer and prettier. When

Jo looked in the mirror, she saw a face with angular lines and domineering features. Big eyes, big mouth, big nose. Her vanity was in her hair, which hung heavily to her shoulders, a honey blond color with only a few strands of gray.

In contrast, Gail's green eyes, dark hair, and even features reminded her of the cheerleaders in high school. Jo was sure she'd been popular. Her outgoing personality and radiant smile hid her dark, moody side.

Gail glanced at the suitcase. "Don't you have any more clothes? I thought you were moving in."

"I can't carry them all at once." Maybe she'd move in slowly, giving them time to adjust before the decision became irrevocable. She'd left the door open at both places.

Backing off a little, Gail studied her. "You sure?"

She shrugged. "As sure as anyone can be." Despite her injured ribs, desire reared its head when Gail gathered her close. She'd never known the passion she felt for this woman. It rivaled the confusing sexual longings of her youth. She cupped Gail's breasts. "Want to celebrate?"

"Later. Let's have a glass of wine." Gail took her hands away and held them briefly. "Now I have to fix dinner. You can help."

Jo made a salad while she sipped the wine. She'd only talked to Gail once since that furtive phone call in the night. "When's Connie coming back?"

"Sunday. I told her you'd be here over the weekend. I wasn't sure you were moving in, though."

"She'll be thrilled to hear that I am," she remarked dryly.

"It's all very hard for her right now," Gail said. "She's always having to pack up and go to her father's. Her school friends live around here."

"And now her mother's lover is moving in." She backed off, warned by Gail's tone. "I understand."

"I wish you had kids. Then you'd get it."

Her kids would at least be polite. Like Mark's son, Ted.

There was something to be said for good manners. "You're right. Do you want me to go back home now or Sunday?"

Gail sent peelings flying into the sink. "I don't ever want you to leave. I just ask you to be patient with Connie. Give her a chance."

Some of the tension drained. "Sure. Whatever."

"I'm sorry. I don't know what's wrong with me."

"I can guess," Jo said, moving to comfort her.

"What then?" Gail asked.

"You're feeling a little threatened about my moving in."

That elicited a wry smile. "Did you diagnose Mark like this? Doesn't he have a kid from his first marriage?"

She grinned and poured more wine. Ted had never called her Mom. At times he'd called her Stepmom. "Yep. No problems there."

Gail's mouth twisted. "I know Connie's difficult. You have to look past that and see the person underneath. She loves animals and books and her friends and me and her dad. Give her a chance and she'll love you, too."

"Of course I'll give her a chance." She didn't hold out much hope for winning Connie's affection, nor did she much care. She just wanted the girl to be civil to her.

They sat down to dinner. Gail enjoyed spending her spare time in the kitchen. Not Jo. The dinners she prepared were easy and quick. She'd have to watch her weight now that she was eating at Gail's.

Gail steered the conversation to safer subjects, like their jobs. She worked for an insurance company, handling clients' claims, which were often outrageous and funny. Jo worked for Temp, Inc. She interviewed prospective employees and fielded calls from companies looking for temporary help.

"Can we hold off till morning?" Gail asked as she filled the dishwasher.

Disappointed again, she asked, "Why?"

"You're still hurting, and I'm kind of tired."

Jo stood at the sink, washing the pans. Was this how it was going to be? Was she too eager, too demanding? When they'd first hooked up, Gail had been as willing as she was, but she wasn't Gail's first woman. Gail was hers. She shrugged. She wasn't sure how she'd manage with her ribs hurting anyway. And she told herself she didn't want it if Gail didn't. But she did.

The next morning she wakened to the slam of the front door. Connie, she thought, coming home early. Damn. She turned her head toward Gail. "Someone's here."

"Mom," a voice called.

Gail leaped out of bed and pulled a robe over her nightshirt, fastening it with a tie. She yelled, "Just a minute, honey."

Connie knocked on the bedroom door, then opened it. The girl's face darkened when she saw Jo. Her mouth twisted in disgust. "This is so sick."

"Come on, Connie." Gail gently pushed her daughter into the hallway and followed, closing the door. Jo watched the lovemaking go out into the hall with them. Fuck.

Lying quietly for a few minutes, she tried to decide whether she should get up, repack her bag, and leave. Then Gail came back.

Gail whispered, "She forgot her homework. She's going back to her dad's. He's waiting in the car."

"Tell her to stay. I'll go." She got up carefully and dressed in the clothes she'd dropped on the floor the previous night.

Gail grabbed her arm. "Don't."

Don't what? she wondered. "What do you want me to do? Hide until she leaves?" Gail said nothing. "All right, all right."

She picked up her book, her ears straining for sounds of Connie leaving. She heard Gail plead and Connie shout. The front door slammed, and a car engine started outside. When Gail returned, Jo tried out a smile.

Gail appeared distracted. "It seems I can't do anything right. When you have a kid, you don't have a life of your own. You know that?"

"Come here." She lifted her arms to Gail, wanting to feel her softness and warmth. Gail came to her then, and she cuddled her stiff body against her own. It only hurt a little.

A small, injured cry burbled out of Gail. "I've been a good mother. I don't deserve this."

"Shhh," she soothed, running a hand over the rigidly curved back, then working it under Gail's nightshirt. "I know something that'll make you feel better."

Gail sniffed and laughed a little. "I bet I can guess what that is."

"A little kissing." She found Gail's lips with hers, which were still swollen and warm from sleep. Their tongues engaged in a little duel.

Struggling out of her nightshirt, Gail wriggled close enough so that their breasts and bellies touched.

"Your ribs. I don't want to hurt you," Gail said.

"It's worth it," she murmured, then gasped with pain when she pulled off her undershirt and panties.

"Hey, we don't have to do this," Gail whispered.

"We can't stop now." Even in the throes of climax, there was discomfort. She ignored it.

When Connie walked through the front door late Sunday afternoon and saw Jo reading alone in the living room, she paused in the doorway. "Why are you still here?"

In the past Jo would have already gone home. "It's good to see you too," she said.

The girl stared at her for a moment before letting out a snort. "Well, it's definitely not good to see you."

Gail came down the hall from the kitchen. "Hi, honey."

"What's she doing here?" Connie gestured at Jo.

"I told you last week, she's going to live with us."

Connie gave them both a glare and brushed past her mother on her way up the stairs. "Maybe I'll go live with Dad."

Gail's hands worked at each other as she gave Jo an imploring look.

"I can leave. It might be better," Jo offered.

Straightening her back, Gail said, "No. She can't always have her way."

This unfriendly atmosphere didn't bode well for their future. "Let it go for now." Maybe Connie would move in with her father, but Gail had told her Connie's dad had a new family. She only went there reluctantly. For a brief moment she felt sorry for the kid. She must feel unimportant in her parents' lives.

She stretched out a hand. "Need some help with dinner?"

Gail said, "Sure."

Connie refused to come down to dinner, but Jo heard her rummaging around downstairs after they'd gone to bed. Smells of warming chicken drifted up the stairs. Anyone else and she'd have joined her for a snack.

IV

Jo felt like a thief, letting herself into the house over the noon hour on Monday to pack another suitcase. She was only taking clothes.

"What are you doing?"

She spun around, hand to chest, and winced at the sudden pain. "Packing a few things."

"You left without telling me you weren't coming back." Mark stood in the doorway, hands on hips.

"I couldn't do what you wanted me to do, and I didn't know how to tell you."

He moved further into the room, still between her and the door. Anger etched lines on his face. "You should have told me."

"You didn't want to listen." She'd never been able to convince him to see her point of view. He would talk right over her, sometimes changing her mind, silencing her. She gave up trying to explain herself. "It's always been that way."

"Is it terrible to want you to stay?" he snapped.

"No, but I can't." She swung the suitcase off the bed.

He threw her on the quilt and fell on her. "I love you."

She let out a little screech of pain. It happened so quickly, was so out of character for him. "You're hurting me."

He backed off the bed and straightened his suit. "Don't sneak in here and take things when I'm gone."

Getting up, she said, "When should I come?"

"Call me first." He stared her down. "That's the least you can do."

Trembling, she walked past him through the familiar house that was no longer hers. They'd lived here fifteen years, had it built to their specifications, moved in a year after they married. She knew he was standing at the top of the stairs as she headed toward the front door and escape.

"Go on, run away," he yelled.

She turned, aware of the hurt in his anger. "You'll find someone who can give you what you want, Mark. I'm just not that person." Then she was out the door, wishing she could abandon her things.

At work, she stepped inside the air conditioned building and paused. The receptionist greeted her.

"Hi, Carol. What have you got for me?"

"Three applicants. Here's the paper work." Carol nodded toward the people sitting in the lobby, paging through magazines. "Three Rivers is looking for a temporary data processer. Smith and Forrester wants someone to research a case." She smiled, showing white teeth lined up in a straight row.

Jo took the forms and notes with her to the women's room and straightened her suit. Running a tongue over her slightly crooked eyeteeth, she compared her set of choppers to Carol's.

Her own were more interesting, she decided. Perfection can be dull. What a joke!

In her office, she looked through her files, called the two businesses, confirming their needs and assuring the personnel department that she'd fill the temporary positions. She located two people who were able to do the work and happy to get it.

Walter Agee knocked on the door and poked his head inside. She looked up, the receiver at her ear, and gestured him inside with a smile. He lowered his bulk into the chair on the other side of the desk and set a cup of coffee in front of her. There was a grace about him despite his excessive weight.

Hanging up, she grinned. "Afternoon."

"We've got to quit meeting this way," he joked. They met this way every weekday and compared notes on the business he had started twenty years ago.

When he left, she called the applicants in one at a time. Always surprised at what people wore to an interview, especially the younger crowd, she studied the woman in front of her who was in her twenties and wore jeans. At least they were clean.

"Your experience is in data processing?" she asked. "I see you scored well on the tests." This woman should be able to find work. Companies were always in need of data processors.

"I've got two kids. I can't afford child care, not on eight dollars an hour. I can only work when my mother takes the kids, which is when she gets home from her job at three."

Affordable child care was a problem Jo couldn't solve. "Where are they now, your children?" she asked.

"With their grandpa but he has to leave at two." The woman glanced at her watch.

"I'll put you on file."

"I really need a job," the woman said.

"I'll do my best. Data processors are always in demand,"

Jo assured her. The hours were the problem. Maybe one of the hospitals needed someone. She made a note to inquire.

A young man, dressed in worn jeans and needing a shave, slouched into her office next. He slumped into the chair in front of her desk, while she studied his application form. She didn't get many men looking for temporary work. Most temp jobs were secretarial and went to women.

Looking at him over the frames of her reading glasses, she said, "You're looking for part time work driving?"

His face lit up. "I like to drive."

"Do you have a commercial license and a clean driving record?"

He frowned. "I just want to do deliveries."

"You need the proper license, then we'll see what can be done. Have you had any citations?" When he looked blank, she said, "Tickets, fines, accidents?"

He shook his head.

The third person was a woman her age, who had been given a pink slip at one of the paper mills after she'd put in twenty years in their packaging department. "I gave them half my life and what do I get out of it?"

"Have you tried the other mills?" Jo asked.

"Nobody wants to hire someone my age for mill work. Besides, my back's giving out."

"I can find you temporary work. Filing, taking inventory, clerking, but nothing will pay like you're accustomed to."

"I don't care," the woman said. "I'm tired. I need a break." She did look old before her time, Jo thought, sort of washed out.

The rest of the day flew by in phone calls, more interviews, finding the right person for a job.

After work, she drove to Gail's in a daze and parked under the overhang. The garage fit only one car.

Letting herself in the side door that opened onto the kitchen, she walked through the tiny dining room into the living room and up the stairs. No sign of Gail. Loud music came from behind Connie's closed door. As Jo paused at the top of the stairs, the door cracked open and a large gray cat leaped through the gap and sped past her down the steps. Connie rushed after it.

She watched the girl and the cat disappear around a corner. Connie called, "Here kitty, kitty."

Lifting her eyebrows in mild surprise, she went into the bedroom she shared with Gail. There were only the two bedrooms upstairs. The spare room downstairs Gail used as an office. Taking off her suit, she crammed it in the full closet, then pulled on a pair of jeans and a T-shirt.

A knock sounded and she opened the door. Connie was clutching the squirming feline, which looked at Jo with wild eyes. "Where'd you get the cat?"

"Don't tell Mom, okay?" Connie said.

"She'll find out. Mothers usually do." Her own mother had never been interested enough to pry. Kimberly and she were always feeding strays until they found them homes. "You have to be careful about cat scratches and bites, you know. They carry some kind of fever."

"You won't tell?" Connie persisted, gripping the struggling cat tighter.

"I won't tell. I won't even hint." She put out a hand to pet the cat and was rewarded with a bite. "Ouch! Is this animal wild?"

"He's been hanging around a lot under the porch."

A door downstairs opened and closed. Gail was home, calling, "Hello."

"Look, animals don't like loud music, unless it's classical. I read that somewhere. Maybe that's why kitty's trying to escape."

"I'll turn it down." Connie vanished into her room.

Just in time. Gail was coming up the stairs. "You beat me home," she said.

"Yep." Jo closed their bedroom door and took Gail in her arms. "You smell wonderful." Sniffing at Gail's hair, she kissed her. One kiss led to two before she backed Gail toward the bed.

Gail laughed and twisted out of her arms. "Not now. I hear Connie's music. She's home."

"Does that mean we can only do it when she's not?" she asked.

"Yes, it does," Gail said, wrinkling her brow. "Are you serious? Do you want her to walk in on us?"

She knew Connie would steer clear of her mother today, but kept her mouth shut.

After supper, Connie usually messed around on the computer or watched a little TV. This night she cleared the table, filled the dishwasher, and went upstairs. "Homework. A test tomorrow," she said when her mother looked perplexed.

On Friday, Jo lunched with Kimberly at the Pub and Grill. Kimberly listened while she told her what had happened with Mark.

"So he got a little emotional. He's entitled," Kim said over her coffee cup.

"He's never lost control like that before. It was kind of scary, being thrown on the bed."

"Maybe it was calculated to show how much he cares. Brad says he's destroyed by this."

"You told Brad?" she asked.

"I didn't tell him you were gay. I told him you moved out. He was flabbergasted. Now he looks at me whenever he thinks I'm not watching."

"How are the kids?" Jo asked.

"Giving me fits. I think I'll be glad when they can drive themselves around. I've become a chauffeur." Kimberly leaned forward. "Listen, Jo. You can't abandon your clothes, your wedding gifts, the things handed down through the family. Mom called last night. Mark told her you'd moved out."

"Nice of him," she said dryly.

"She wanted to know why, when you had it so cushy." Kimberly raised her hands as if to ward off Jo's alarm. "I didn't tell her."

"Well, I'm not going to tell her either. She doesn't have to know. I mean, she never comes back here." She could keep this secret from her mother. Why upset her? Her mother's only passions were golf and bridge. Jo wasn't sure she thought about anything else.

"She coughed and coughed. I thought she was going to choke to death," Kim said.

"She won't quit smoking. She'll die with a cigarette between her lips."

"She's hooked," Kimberly agreed, "and she didn't sound good."

Their sandwiches arrived. They paused to eat a few bites. "How are your ribs?" Kimberly asked between swallows.

"Better."

"How are you getting along with the girl?"

"Connie? She was hiding a cat in her room the other night and asked me to keep it secret. It looked wild to me, all claws and balls. It'll tear her room apart."

"You didn't tell Gail?" Kimberly's eyes probed hers.

"I didn't tell." She smiled a little. If Connie wanted a cat that much, maybe Gail would let her have this one.

"My kids would all have their own pet if we let them. Already it's a zoo with the dog, the cat, and the rabbit."

Jo laughed. "We never had a pet. Remember? Mother didn't want hair in the house. Mark's son, Ted, used to bring his dog when he came on his visits. It was such a cutie. They were inseparable." She might never see Ted again.

V

How she loved the weekends Connie spent at her dad's. Two nights and days without the girl hanging around looking put-upon. She strode to her car with a lighter step. She'd get home early, she thought, opening the door. She felt guilty every time she slid behind the wheel of the Chrysler convertible Mark had given her as an anniversary gift. He was driving a rental.

Parking under the overhang next to Gail's house made her think she should give it back. It shouldn't be left out in the weather.

Letting herself in the side door, she heard the beat of Connie's radio. Damn, she thought, dropping her purse next to the davenport and walking toward the stairs. Shoes abandoned on the first step, a jacket thrown over the bannister.

Knocking on Connie's door, she pressed her ear against the wood. Maybe Connie had left the radio on to hide the cat's cries of distress. It apparently hated captivity. Connie seemed determined to not only keep it but hide it from her mother.

The door opened so suddenly she nearly fell inside. Catching her balance, she spied the cat peering out from under the bed. It launched itself toward freedom as Connie stepped into the hall and shut the door in its face. She heard a little thud. "I have to keep the music on. Mom'll hear it."

"Are you going to take it to your dad's tonight?" She backed up a few steps to put a little space between herself and the girl.

Connie looked desperate. "I can't. Dad has a dog. I'll have to stay home."

Oh no, she thought. "I'll take the cat to my sister's house for the weekend. She has a cat. What's one more?"

"Mom's going to be home any minute," Connie said.

"Put him in a box and carry him downstairs to my car. I'll go right now."

"Thanks," Connie said, disappearing into her room and emerging with a box. The cat's head stuck out of the flaps, one ear flattened, as it struggled to escape.

She looked at the animal and changed her mind. She couldn't foist a wild cat on Kim. "I'll tell you what. Why don't I take it to the vet instead? It needs to be neutered, to have its front claws pulled, to have necessary shots."

Connie's eyes widened in alarm. "Pull its claws," she shrieked.

"It'll tear up the furniture if you don't. They'll anesthetize it first."

The girl looked thoughtful for a moment. "What do you mean neuter?"

Jo was getting impatient. "Cut its balls off. It'll stop yowling so much then. Look, do you want a pet or a wild animal?"

A car passed in the street and they both paused and listened for it to turn in the driveway. "Come on, Connie. If we're going to do this, we have to do it now. Make up your mind."

"I don't have any money," Connie admitted.

"I do." Grabbing the box from the girl, she tucked the cat's head inside and hurried down the stairs with Connie following. Putting the cat in the box on the front seat, she slammed the door and galloped to the driver's side. Already the cat's head and shoulders were emerging from the loosely shut container.

She shoved the animal back in the box, getting bitten and clawed in the process, started the engine, and backed out of the driveway. Taking another route than the one Gail took home, she drove to the nearest veterinary clinic, praying it would be open.

The cat was shredding her hand, the one that held it in the box. "Ouch, you lousy son of a bitch. Pretty soon you won't feel so macho."

Dragging the box out of her side of the car, she carried it to the door which a woman with a dog at her side shut on her way out. The sign in the window read Closed. "You're not, are you?"

"What have you got in the box?" The woman smiled, putting a hand on the large dog's head.

"A cat that needs to be civilized. He's going to escape any minute, and I'll never be forgiven if he runs into the road and kills himself."

The woman laughed. She was taller than Jo with gray eyes and high cheekbones. Curls cascaded down her back. Her ears were small and close to her head.

The cat grabbed Jo's hand with its claws and teeth and bit hard. "Ahhh," she yelled.

"Come on in. You need a kennel for that animal," The woman opened the door of the pickup truck for the dog and unlocked the door of the clinic.

Once inside, Jo let go of the cat and held the flaps down. "Will you keep him over the weekend and neuter and declaw him? I'm in a real bind." She couldn't very well admit that her lover's daughter was hiding the cat from her mother, that the girl hated her, and this might be a way to gain a little of the kid's trust.

"I'm Laura Bender, one of the vets. I'll be the only one here tomorrow, so I can't do anything with the cat until Monday. What's his name?" Laura hauled down a kennel and dumped the bellowing cat inside, then latched the door. "There," she said. "That works better than a box." She turned to shake Jo's hand and said instead, "We better doctor your hand."

Jo went limp with relief. "I can't thank you enough."

"You'll pay for it." Laura took out a medicine kit from under the counter and disinfected Jo's hand, then wrapped it with gauze. "Let's fill out some paperwork before you go." Laura looked up, her gaze clear and calm. "Name, address, telephone, cat's name and age."

Jo threw her hands in the air. "We haven't named him yet." She gave the other information. "He's kind of a surprise. If you don't get me, just leave a number and I'll call back."

Laura carried the cat to the back where large kennels lined the aisles. She transferred Connie's cat to one of these. The cat was crouched in a corner, hissing his displeasure and fear, when Laura closed the door.

"He should be ready to pick up Monday afternoon." She winked. "He'll be okay. He's just scared."

Jo backed out of the front door, so grateful she nearly bowed. She felt bonded with this woman. On the drive home she tried to remember Laura's hands. Had there been a ring on the left one?

She drove into the driveway as Connie climbed into an

Expedition parked by the curb. The girl hesitated, then said something to the man inside and hurried to the Sebring.

"He'll be ready to be picked up Monday afternoon," Jo said, getting out of the convertible.

"What happened to your hand?" Connie asked. "Did he do that?"

Blood was seeping through the gauze. She'd have to think of something to tell Gail. "I'll live. We'll talk Sunday night."

"About what?" the girl asked.

"The cat. Where he came from, how to introduce him to your mother." Gail was opening the side door. She would be suspicious of any friendly conversation between her daughter and Jo, who waved her hand as if to shoo Connie away. But she had to lay the groundwork. "You better go."

"Hey, what's happening?" Gail asked, watching her daughter head for the Expedition. She was apparently distracted by the vehicle. "No way could I afford an SUV. I should have asked for a better settlement."

"Why would you want one? They're gas guzzlers," Jo said.

"I know." Gail continued to watch the Expedition as it drove away. "I just want to be able to afford one."

Jo would call Mark tonight and get the Chrysler off her conscience. She told Gail her plans as they went inside.

"Why shouldn't you keep the car? It was a gift," Gail said.

"An anniversary gift." She reached for Gail in the tiny kitchen. "We're alone. How about a little quickie?"

"How about a little drinkie first?"

"Okay. I'll fix them. But let's sit down and talk some before we eat," she said as Gail tied an apron over her jeans.

They sat side by side on the couch facing the TV. "What happened?" Gail asked, taking Jo's injured hand between her own.

Jo pulled it away. "I caught it in the desk drawer. It looks worse than it feels."

"Maybe we should rewrap it," Gail said.

"It's okay. I'll take care of it later." Jo took a deep breath and told herself a white lie wasn't a bad thing. "Someone at work has a cat she has to unload, because her husband is allergic to it. I thought maybe we could take it in. It'd be a pet for Connie."

Gail looked at her. "I thought you didn't like cats, that you loved dogs."

"As long as cats are kept inside, they're okay. When they're allowed to run outside, they kill everything they catch. I do prefer dogs, but I hate to see the cat put down, and that's probably what will happen to it. It's not a kitten."

"Somebody's pet, huh?" Gail said slowly.

The drink helped. She pictured the cat Connie had brought into the house. Its yellow eyes could have belonged to a bobcat. She nodded.

The next morning she awoke slowly. Gail's warm body lay tucked into her side. With a thumb she straightened the fierce wrinkles between Gail's eyes and watched her eyelids flicker open. "What were you dreaming? You looked crabby."

"It's gone. Can't retrieve it." Gail snuggled closer. "Mmm. We have the whole day together."

"Yeah, well, let's start it out right." She got on top, her favorite position, and smiled down at Gail. "Wanna?" She kissed Gail, inhaling the scent of her. Her lips were always delicious in the morning, soft, warm.

"I should brush my teeth," Gail murmured.

"No, you shouldn't," she said, although she was sucking on a breath mint taken from a roll under her pillow. She tongued it into Gail's mouth.

Sliding to the side, she freed a hand to stroke the curves and planes of Gail's body. Gail was always dieting, but Jo loved her softness, the womanly curves a little extra weight emphasized. Sliding under the sheet, she tasted a breast, feeling the nipple harden. She smiled at the small gasp provoked when her fingers plunged inside, felt the inner walls swell and the fluids begin to flow. She became wet.

Gail tugged gently on her arms, trying to pull her up where she could reach her.

"Not yet," Jo whispered, her mouth full of breast, thinking this was how she liked it. Being in control.

Slowly, they moved toward climax. It always made Jo a little sad to realize that it would soon be over, but prolonging orgasm when they were both almost there only lessened it. Lowering herself onto Gail, she shuddered at the warm touch of tongue. Then it was over.

Reversing her position, she smiled into Gail's eyes and wondered how they could do what they did to each other and go back to normal behavior. Soon they'd be sitting at the table, drinking morning coffee, reading the paper as if the intense intimacy had never happened.

They didn't look at cars as planned. When she called Mark, he said, "I gave you that car. Don't you want it?"

"I was trying to save you from having to buy a new vehicle," she said. He was taking her gesture as an insult.

"You were trying to assuage your guilt," he shot back. "The insurance will buy me a new one."

VI

They drove to High Cliff State Park to hike. The leaves on the aspens and maples were various shades of yellow and red. Standing at the top of the escarpment, they watched climbers rappel its steep rocky walls. A warm wind played with Jo's hair, lifting it off her forehead as if it were alive.

On the trail, a golden retriever bounded ahead of its owners, greeting them with lolling tongue. "Don't jump on me," Gail said, warding the dog off with outstretched hands.

The animal turned to Jo, who patted the dog as best she could as it jumped around her. "Nice pooch. Good dog," she crooned.

After the owners corralled the dog and moved past them in the other direction, she said, "Have you thought more about giving that cat a home?" Gail looked cute, her cheeks reddened by wind and sun.

"Connie's dad has a dog. He sheds all over everything and sneaks up on the furniture whenever he can. He smells, too."

"Well, maybe cats don't smell. I never had one."

"I never liked cats much," Gail said. "There's something sneaky about them."

What would she do with this cat if Gail wouldn't accept it? "Cats are just independent." The breeze filtered through the trees, spinning the leaves. A few fluttered down to brighten the bark strewn pathway.

Gail looked at her curiously. "How soon does this woman have to unload the cat?"

"Monday. They've been keeping it in the basement." Another lie.

"Can't she take it to the Humane Association?"

"It'll probably be destroyed. They've got so many cats."

Gail glanced at her, narrowing her eyes. "All right," she said, "but it's on probation. If it pees in corners, we're getting rid of it."

Relieved, Jo said, "Oh, I agree."

"What's its name?" Gail asked after a small silence.

"I don't remember. Something like Boo Boo." It was as good a name as any, although it didn't fit the feral animal.

Before Connie went to bed Sunday, Jo followed the girl upstairs. She spoke quickly and quietly. "I talked your mom into giving the cat a trial run. She thinks it's a housecat that someone at work had to give away. His name is Boo Boo. Okay? He's supposed to be a surprise for you."

Connie's face lit up. She opened her mouth.

Jo put a finger to her own lips. "Keep them sealed. I'll pick Boo Boo up after work tomorrow."

"Can I go with you?" Connie whispered.

"Better not. I'd have to come home first and your mom might want to come with us. I don't want her to know I lied about all this." Why had she lied? Gail might have agreed to take the cat in anyway.

A cold drizzle fell all of Monday. Mondays were bad enough without rain, Jo thought as she hurried into the clinic at five fifteen. If Gail reached out a friendly hand and the cat bit it, that might be all the probation the animal got. Oh well, she'd tried.

The two women behind the reception counter looked up and smiled. She walked past several people waiting with their dogs and cats. The dogs panted nervously, occasionally whining their worry. The cats hissed and meowed with distress.

She gave her name, and one of the women went to get the cat. The other said, "Dr. Bender left a half hour ago. She said to tell you to call if you have any problems. The cat came out of surgery fine. He's still a little sleepy."

"What do I need for this cat? I have nothing."

"Well, a litter box and litter, cat food, all of which we sell. Right now he needs this special litter, because of his feet."

Carrying out the purchases and stashing them in the backseat, she returned to pay the bill and fetch the cat. She mentally gasped. Nearly two hundred dollars. Writing out a check, she hoped it would pay off by bringing peace to the house.

Crouched in the kennel, Boo Boo's pitiful meows grew in volume as she drove. She dreaded turning the animal loose in Gail's neat little house. Connie would have to take him to her room, she decided, as she pulled into Gail's drive and parked under the overhang.

Connie flew out the door as Jo opened her door. Before the girl could carry the kennel with the unhappy cat into the house, she grabbed the girl's arm and whispered fiercely, "Take him up to your room. I've got everything he needs here. Is your mom home?"

"Yeah. She's in the kitchen."

Goodie, she thought, stepping out under the overhang

where the wet wind swept up her pantslegs. She put the bags of food and litter into the plastic litter box and carried it into the warm, steamy kitchen.

"Hi, sweetie," she said, hurrying past Gail.

"Why are you both in such a rush? I barely saw the cat."

"Well, it might have to pee or poop. I'm taking this stuff up to Connie's room."

"Gimme a kiss," Gail said, smiling at her. "Connie is so excited."

"I know." Jo went on through the house and climbed the stairs. She set her armload down to knock on Connie's door. "Let me in."

She had never been in Connie's room before. It was small and packed with furniture. The comforter on the bed held many stuffed animals. It was easy to forget that Connie wasn't much more than a child.

The cat keened from the kennel. Connie stood over it, looking wary. "Should I let it go?"

"Let's first put some food and water down and fill its litter box."

Connie opened the kennel door with trepidation. Jo realized the girl was worried about how Boo Boo would behave.

The cat stepped out of the cage gingerly, his front feet bloodied. He staggered past them, and tottered toward the open door. Connie picked him up and burst into tears. "Look at his feet. What have they done to him?"

Jo stood speechless with horror. The animal's toes were mutilated. "What will I tell your mother?"

"Why did you do this to him?" Connie sobbed. "Poor thing."

"I didn't," she said. "I'll call the clinic. Maybe there's some pain medication."

She left Connie cradling the cat and went to Gail's bedroom to phone. "This poor animal looks like he's been tortured," she said when someone answered. It was only a woman from the answering service who could tell her nothing.

"Should I have one of the vets call you?"

"I'll call tomorrow." She hung up and went back to Connie's room.

The girl was sitting on her bed, the cat in her lap. She gave Jo a dirty look. "I knew I couldn't trust you."

"I'm off to get some baby aspirin. Surely he can handle that."

She found Gail in the kitchen opening a can of tuna fish. "Just a little getting acquainted treat for Boo Boo. Why don't you bring his stuff down here. We can put the litter box in the mud room and his food and water in the kitchen."

"He's a little indisposed right now. The vet pulled his claws. It hadn't been done."

Connie's horror was mirrored in her mother's face. "Poor thing."

"I'm going to get some pain reliever for him."

First thing at work the next day Jo called the clinic and asked for Dr. Bender. "She has the day off," the woman told her. "Would you like to talk to one of the other veterinarians?"

She said, "I picked my cat up last night after having it declawed. He looks like he's been tortured and can hardly walk. I went out and got some baby aspirin, but he's not much better today."

"I know it looks dreadful, but in a few days he'll be fully recovered, and he won't remember. I can let you talk to another doctor."

"That's okay."

Then she called Mark to ask if she could go to the house with Kimberly and get some of her things at noon.

"I can't be there," he said. "I have a lunch meeting."

"Well, is it okay?"

"What are you going to take?"

"My clothes and some other things that are mine. I can't take furniture right now."

"Why don't you come on Saturday morning?"

"I'll call Kim. Her weekends are pretty busy." So he didn't trust her, she thought as she placed the receiver in its cradle.

She'd come in early, intending to catch up on unfinished work. Now she had to call Kim and change their plans.

"Hey, girl, can you help me get my stuff out of the house Saturday morning?"

"I thought we were going in today."

"Mark wants to be there," she explained. "He's got a meeting today."

"Well, it's damn inconvenient," Kim said.

"You don't have to, Kimmie. I can do it alone."

"What time Saturday?"

"Let's meet for breakfast at the diner, nine o'clock." She looked up as Carol stuck her head through the door. "Got to go now."

"Sorry," Carol said, closing the door behind her. "That guy is back, Keith Csyzka. He still hasn't shaved or changed his jeans from the look of him."

"Send him in." She sighed. "I suppose I'll have to tell him how to dress."

"I got the license." He handed it to her like a trophy. "Can you get me a job now? I need spending money."

She had phoned a friend in BMV for his driving record. It was clean. "I'll check around and see what there is. No one's called in asking for a driver. Try the car companies. They need people to shuttle customers and parts."

"I don't want nothing full time," he said.

"Why not?" she asked.

"I don't like no one telling me what to do all the time."

She had been about to tell him how to dress but decided against it.

Kim's brown hair floated around her head in kinky strands. "Like my new do?"

"It's different," Jo said. Kim was always changing her hairstyle.

Over omelets, toast, American fries and coffee, they caught up. "How's the cat?" Kim asked.

"You should have seen his poor bloody feet when I picked him up Monday. I was appalled and Connie blamed me, of course."

Kim nodded. "I felt so guilty when I picked Millie up after the surgery. I should have warned you. Didn't you get any brownie points with Connie for your efforts on behalf of Boo Boo?"

Jo grimaced. "Not after she saw his feet."

"Will she be home when we take your stuff over?" Kim asked. "I'd like to meet her."

"Maybe. It seems like she goes less and less to her dad's on weekends." That too was a bone between her and Gail. They had less time together. "How are the fearsome five?" she asked.

"Why don't you come over and find out? They miss you."

"Invite us, Gail and me, and we'll come. Maybe we'll bring Connie."

"Okay," Kim said. "Just don't bring Boo Boo."

Jo glanced at her watch. "We better get moving."

When Mark flung the front door open, Jo said, "We're here."

"So I see." Mark rocked back on his heels. "Come on in."

In the middle of the living room lay boxes with clothing

heaped on them. Mark gestured. "Your things, all boxed up and ready to go."

She went toward the pile, no longer caring how lost he might feel alone in all this space. Looking through the boxes, she found family wedding presents, the pictures and photos she'd taken, the china and tableware she'd bought before marriage.

He stood over her, his arms crossed. "Everything's there, except the furniture. You'll have to rent a trailer for that. Why don't you come back for it next Saturday?"

She looked up at him. "I want to look around, just to make sure you didn't forget anything."

He followed her and Kim through the many rooms where she peered into half empty closets, cupboards, and dressers. She and Kim crammed her belongings in the two cars without his help.

"Maybe Brad will help us with the furniture," Kim said before they drove off.

But where would she put furniture in Gail's house? There was no room. She'd have to check out the basement.

They unloaded with Gail's help, cramming Jo's clothes into closets and dressers that were already full.

"Do you want any of this stuff, Kim?" she asked her sister about the boxes that didn't hold clothes.

"I can store them for you. I can probably find a place for the furniture, too," Kim said, her glance shifting between the two women. "Let's put what you don't have room for in my car."

"How about some lunch?" Gail suggested. She had just freed Boo Boo from his kennel, where they'd put him so they could leave the outer door open.

Jo looked at the cat rubbing against Kim's leg and shoved him away with a foot. "Stop that, Boo."

"I'm used to it," Kim said. "I feel like a post sometimes. I'll have some coffee if you've got some made. Then I must go."

Jo sat quietly at the table while Gail and Kim chatted. Kids, food, books. Kim invited them both to dinner Friday night. "Bring Connie if she's around. I have five of my own. They're younger, though, and probably louder. Does Connie ever babysit?" she asked, quickly adding, "But I'd feel guilty unleashing five kids on an unsuspecting babysitter."

VII

"I like her," Gail said when Kim was gone.

"I like her too."

"Are you okay, sweetheart? You're so quiet."

Jo smiled at the endearment. They seldom addressed each other except by name for fear of offending Connie. She pulled Gail onto her lap. "I hate the thought of going back to the house to get my furniture next Saturday."

Gail put her arms around Jo's neck. "Then it'll be over, except for the divorce. You had a phone call this morning. Almost forgot to tell you." She fished a note out of her pocket.

"A Dr. Laura Bender. Who's she?" Gail asked.

"The veterinarian who operated on the cat." Her heart

picked up speed. She went into the other room to return the call.

The answering service came on the line for the veterinary clinic. Dr. Bender had left the building at noon, the woman said. Was this an emergency?

"No, I'll call her Monday." She hung up and picked up the Saturday paper. After reading it through , she started on the crossword puzzle.

The phone rang, and Gail called from the kitchen, "Answer it, will you, sweets? My hands are a mess."

It was Kim telling her their mother had called and wanted to talk to her. "Do I have to?"

"Yes, you have to. Just give her a quick call. She wants your phone number and address."

"You could have given her them."

"She wanted to talk to you."

Fuck, she thought as she fumbled through her purse for her address book.

The deep, hoarse voice of her mother rang in her ears as if she were down the block instead of a thousand miles away. Years of smoking had damaged her vocal chords. Jo heard the rasping of her lungs trying to take in enough air. "Ginger Cottrell speaking."

"Hi, Mother."

"JoAnn? It's about time. Why didn't you tell me you were leaving Mark?" Her mother's voice thickened with annoyance.

"I would have. It's not like we talk every week." Every month or two was more like it.

"I don't have your new phone number and address. Let me get something to write on." In the background was the sound of silence. No music. No one talking.

She gave both to her mother, then asked about Stan, her stepfather.

"Mark is destroyed by your leaving."

A nervous laugh bubbled out of her. "No, he's not. I saw

him this morning after he piled my things on the living room floor. He wasn't devastated. He wasn't even polite."

"He sounded so unhappy when I spoke to him."

Her mother preferred men to women. She seemed to favor her daughters' husbands. "He's angry and yes, he has a right to be, and I don't want to talk about it anymore."

"Well, I do, and I'm your mother."

"And I'm forty-two years old," she snapped. Then she felt contrite. "Kim said you had a bad cough."

"I'm better," her mother said.

"Have you quit smoking?"

"None of your business. Don't get smart with me."

"I'm not, Mother. Kim said you wanted to talk to me, so I called."

"I thought you would tell me about something so important as the dissolution of your marriage. I didn't think I'd hear the news from Mark."

"Sorry. I'm not ready to talk about it, is all."

"Well, I know I'm unimportant in your life."

"Mother," she said with annoyance, "I knew you'd be critical. I was working up my courage to tell you."

"That's unfair," her mother snapped.

"No, it's not. That's how it is."

"That's how you see it." And then her mother broke into a cough that went on and on.

"I'm sorry, Mom. Take better care of yourself, will you?"

"I'm not getting any younger," her mother said between alarming gasps.

Jo felt exhausted and was surprised to see streaks of sunshine slanting through the windows behind her when she hung up. It was early afternoon and too nice to be inside.

"I think I'll wash the windows," she told Gail, heading toward the door.

"How nice. I'm fixing something special for dinner," Gail said, kissing her on the cheek in passing.

On the ladder wiping away accumulated grime, she reflected how much time had passed since she'd seen her mother. Once a year she managed a few days in Florida. It always turned out badly.

After a meal of stuffed pork tenderloin with garlic potatoes and roasted carrots, she and Gail moved to the living room couch to watch a video. The cat perched on the back of the sofa behind their heads. No matter how many times Jo put the animal on the floor, he climbed back on the furniture.

Placing an arm around Gail's shoulders, she sighed with pleasure. This was the scenario she'd hoped to live this past year. The movie, Drop Dead Gorgeous, which one of her co-workers had lent Gail, turned out to be a dark comedy. A tasteless spoof on beauty pageants and parents who push their kids to extremes. It also made fun of small town Minnesota.

When she howled with laughter, Gail looked at her with disbelief. "This is sick."

"Of course it is. It's supposed to be."

"What's funny about murder?"

"Don't take it so seriously. It's like Fargo or the Monty Python movies — black comedy."

"I didn't like those either."

"Aw, come on. Some things are just silly, and this is one of them."

When one of the contestants was blown to bits, Gail said, "Explain why that is funny?"

"Turn it off. I'll watch it on my own."

In bed, she listened to the cat crying outside their closed door. Such a small thing, not being amused by the same thing, but it bothered her.

After a few moments, Gail got up and left the room. Jo heard her tell the cat to hush, then carry the animal to Connie's room and shut the door on it.

"What if it has to use the litter box?" she asked when Gail climbed back in bed.

"I can't sleep with it caterwauling outside the door."

"It misses Connie."

"Do you ever miss Connie?" Gail asked.

"Yeah. Especially when the cat's yowling, wanting someone to sleep with."

"That's the only time, I bet."

"Come on, Gail. Why are we fighting?"

"I'll go get his things," Gail said, sitting up.

"No, I will."

She stubbed her toe on a chair in the dark living room and hopped around, cursing. "Goddamn." The whole evening was ruined. Turning on the kitchen light, she picked up the litter box and made her way upstairs. She had to go down again for the cat's water and food. By then she was not the least bit sleepy, so she went back downstairs and finished watching the movie.

Gail was asleep when she slid in bed around midnight. It took her a long time to lose consciousness.

The following night, Jo found Connie curled up on the couch watching the movie. She and Gail had walked in the door from dinner at Gail's friends, Tawnya and Bev, the only other lesbian couple that she knew.

"That's not a movie I'd rather you watch," Gail said.

"Why not? It's funny."

"Isn't it, though?" Jo said, feeling vindicated.

"It's bizarre." Gail walked through the room. "I'm not watching it again."

Jo sat on the other end of the sofa. "Mind if I join you?"

"Suit yourself," the girl said.

"Want some popcorn?" She wasn't trying to suck up to the girl, she told herself, she was still hungry. They'd had tofu something or other for supper.

"Sure," Connie replied, temporarily forgetting her vendetta.

They watched till the end, guffawing at the tasteless

humor. While rewinding the tape, Jo got hooked on a program on public TV. "He missed you," she said when Connie headed toward the stairs with the cat.

Connie hesitated. "How do you know?"

"He tried to sleep with us last night."

"That is sick," Connie remarked.

"If you say so," Jo muttered.

Later, Gail came downstairs to ask when she was coming to bed.

"When this program's done. It's a spy thing. Why don't you watch with me." She patted the cushion and glanced at Gail, taking notice of her tight lips. "What's wrong?"

"I'd appreciate it if you didn't encourage Connie to watch stuff like that movie."

"She didn't take it seriously. At least, she has a sense of humor." Oops. It just slipped out. She'd pay for it.

Gail turned on her heel and stomped upstairs. Jo wrapped herself up in an afghan and spent the night on the couch in restless sleep.

Breakfast was a silent affair. Jo was a morning person, cheerful when she got up, while Gail and Connie dragged themselves around like the living dead. Jo had learned to be quiet until Gail had taken a few sips of coffee. Connie's morning demeanor she chalked up to her age and ignored it.

At work, she listened to her voice mail, met with applicants, returned calls and scanned computer files finding people to fit job requests.

Gail phoned around eleven thirty, wanting to meet for lunch. "I've been calling all morning and just now got through."

"You can always leave a message with Carol. She'll get it to me."

"I want to talk," Gail said.

"What about?" she asked, paging through the messages Carol had just handed her.

"In person."

At the restaurant she sat across from Gail, who still looked annoyed. "Now what have I done?"

"You slept on the couch. You undermined me with Connie."

"You undermined yourself," Jo said. "I fell asleep on the sofa. So what? And if you didn't want Connie to see the movie, you should have told her she couldn't, not blame it on me."

"Well, I can see this is going nowhere," Gail huffed.

"Let's save it for something serious," she said, then reached across the table to touch Gail's tightly clasped hands. Gail snatched them away. Well, this is great, she thought. Already we're fighting about stupid things.

"Why are you so angry? Isn't that what you wanted? Me to get along with Connie? For the three of us to be one happy family?"

Gail hissed, "I don't like it when you sleep on the sofa. If we can't sleep together, why are we living together?"

"Oh, for chrissake," she said. "It was only one night. I'll sleep with you tonight if you'll let me in the bed."

"You are getting along better with Connie, but do you have to do it by defying me?"

"I wasn't defying you," she said.

"Parents stick together when it comes to discipline."

"I'm not her parent, nor does she want me to be," Jo pointed out. "I'd like her to trust and like me a little. That's all."

Gail shrugged. "I guess I should be grateful for that."

VIII

After lunch, she returned Dr. Bender's phone call.

"I was following up on the cat. How is he?"

"Still gimping around. You'd never know he was a wild cat now. It sure slowed him down." She pictured Laura Bender in her white jacket. "I called the clinic after I picked him up. We were horrified by his bloody paws."

"It's a pretty barbaric thing to do, I agree, but the alternative is shredded furniture and drapes and flesh."

"I know. I was afraid he'd revert to his feral self, but he hasn't. Yet. Thanks to you."

"Once they're neutered, male cats make good pets."

Jo kept talking, keeping the woman on the line. "When do you think I should bring him in again?"

"In a year, for his boosters. We'll send a card to remind you," Laura said.

"Oh. There isn't a follow-up exam after the surgery? No stitches to come out?"

"None of that, but you can bring him in Saturday morning. I'll be here."

"Okay, thanks," she said. "See you then."

"Good. Maybe you'll tell me the story behind the cat."

"I will." Jo smiled at the receiver after hanging up and then remembered the furniture she was supposed to move Saturday morning. Oh well, she could do that in the afternoon.

The week flew by. After work on Friday, she bought a bottle of Bogle Merlot on her way home and pulled in under the overhang ten minutes later than usual.

She found Gail and Connie arguing in the kitchen. From the angry exchange of words, she gathered there was a last minute overnight party at someone's house and Connie wanted to go. Gail was saying that Kim expected all three of them for dinner

Jo broke in. "Hey, it doesn't matter. Kim will be disappointed if Connie doesn't go, but there's always another time." She leaned against the counter, relieved. What would Connie do for entertainment when the four grown-ups were talking and Kim's kids vanished into their rooms? Or worse, latched onto her? The oldest, Max, was ten. At his age he'd be likely to avoid her. The next oldest was Lauren, who was only eight. Then came the six year old twins, Anna and Ben. The baby, Sydney, was four.

Gail glared at her. "That isn't the point, Jo. She has to learn when you make a commitment, you keep it."

The last thing she wanted was for the girl to go along with

them against her will. No one sulked better than Connie. "Can I talk to you, Gail?"

Connie took the opportunity to escape to her room. "I have to change."

"Let her go to the party, Gail. She'll probably be bored at Kim's."

"I thought Kim had five kids."

"Yeah, but they're all younger." She rattled off their genders and ages. "Max is the only one close in age and he thinks girls are sissies to be avoided."

"All right," Gail said.

When they drove Connie to the friend's house where she was spending the night, Gail told her daughter that Jo was taking the cat to the vet the next morning.

"What time?" Connie asked.

"Nine," Jo replied, hoping the girl wouldn't want to come along.

"I wanna go too."

Jo glanced in the rearview mirror and tried to discourage her. "It's just a routine follow-up."

"Please?"

Jo and Gail continued on to Kim's house. The day had been wet with periodic bouts of rain. It was difficult to see the road's dividing line once they were out of the city.

Kim and Brad's house was a two story brick with an attached sun porch and three car garage. When they pulled into the driveway, motion sensor lights came on, focusing on them.

Gail muttered, "Big place."

"Big family," Jo said. "No need to lock the car." She got out of her side as the twins barrelled around the corner of the house and threw themselves at her. Barney barked at their heels.

She hugged each in turn and introduced them to Gail.

"Want to play kick the can?" Anna asked, her little face flushed with excitement. "Lauren's it."

"I think we'd better say hello to your mom. Where is she?"

"In the kitchen," Ben hollered as they ran across the lawn and hid behind the yews out front. Barney followed, disappearing into the shrubbery with the twins.

Jo led Gail around the side of the house to the kitchen door and went in through the mud room, calling, "Here we are."

Kim turned from the stove where she was stirring something and sipping wine. She lifted the glass. "Want one? Or would you like something more potent?"

"Vodka and tonic," she said. "I'll fix it."

"And you, Gail?" Kim inquired.

"The wine looks good," Gail replied.

"Did Connie get waylaid outside?"

"No, she went to a last minute party. Jo said you'd understand."

"Of course. She probably would've been bored. Max is spending the night at his buddy's house down the road. Couldn't get rid of Lauren and the twins. In fact, Lauren's friend, Julie, is staying overnight here. Sit down and keep me company."

"Can I help?" Gail asked.

"Nope. Everything's under control," Kim responded.

"Kim's efficiency is frightening. Trust me, we'd only get in the way." Jo perched on a stool at the counter. "Where's the man of the house?"

"Brad? He had to meet with some clients who are protesting the building of a factory dairy farm in their rural neighborhood."

Jo was immediately suspicious. "Will he be home for dinner?" She worried he might be avoiding her and Gail.

"Yes." Kim belted back the wine. "Pour me some more."

They sat down to eat at the long mahogany table. Kim at one end and a just arrived Brad at the other. Jo smiled across the table at Gail, who had been placed next to the two giggling girls, Lauren and Julie. Ben and Anna squirmed on either side of Jo, each demanding her attention. Sydney was already in bed.

"It's rude to giggle at the table," Kim said sternly, which only caused Lauren and Julie to snort as they tried to subdue their laughter and then burst into more gales of hilarity.

"I'm used to girls," Gail said, smiling at the two next to her, causing them to erupt with mirth.

Jo tried to imagine Connie giggling uncontrollably, and failed. "So how'd the factory farm thing go?" she asked Brad.

"Have you ever driven past a farm where the manure of a hundred cows has been piled or spread on the fields? Multiply a hundred cows by twenty five, and that's the problem they're going to have here. The logistics of disposing of that much excrement without polluting the air and ground water are scary. Not only that, they'll need huge amounts of clean water. And there'll be umpteen dozen milk trucks entering and leaving all day long."

Gail began to ask questions about the proposed factory farm. "What are their chances of getting a permit from the DNR?"

"Pretty good, I think."

"What will their operation do to the smaller dairy farms?"

"Mega competition," he said. "Eventually these huge farms will probably drive the smaller family farms out of business. But now tell us what you do for a living. It has to be better than this."

Gail regaled them with clients' accident reports. Jo had heard about trees that supposedly jumped out in front of headlights on a dark night, about dogs putting the owner's car or truck in gear, about vehicles abandoned then reported as stolen. "People believe they're entitled to collect just because they paid in."

After dinner the kids went outside again to play kick the can. Brad took Jo aside and told her she needed to hire an attorney to handle the divorce.

"But we haven't started divorce proceedings," she said, "and Mark's an attorney. Can't he take care of it?"

"You need your own lawyer." He studied her face. "I can recommend a fine woman attorney who does mostly divorces. Audrey Compton."

"Thanks, Brad," she said.

The next morning Jo dragged herself out of bed before eight, showered, and ate a piece of toast. Corralling the cat in a corner, she thrust him in the kennel as Gail came into the kitchen.

"You should have woke me up. I would have gone with you. Now it's too late."

"You looked so peaceful. I'll be back after we see the vet and then I'm meeting Kim at Mark's. I'll pick up the rental truck at noon."

Boo Boo's complaints rose to a wail that lifted the hairs on the back of her neck. She gave Gail a quick kiss, grabbed the kennel, and scuttled toward the door. "Got to go."

Parking outside the house where they'd left Connie the previous night, she rang the front doorbell — twice. Hearing it echo inside, she stood patiently for four minutes, timed by her watch, then walked back to her car.

"Hey, wait up. I'm coming."

"Connie?" she asked. "Is that you?"

"Who else? Let me get my stuff. I'll be right out."

Sliding behind the wheel of the Chrysler, Jo waited. The cat meowed loudly in the back, poking its pathetic paws through the kennel bars. When the passenger door opened and Connie threw herself in the front seat, Jo started the engine.

"Do you like it?" Connie asked, sounding hopeful.

She studied the girl's newly blond hair. It was a home job, not very well done. She couldn't tell such a blatant lie. "I liked it better natural."

Connie slumped against the back of the seat. "I hate it. I want to change it back."

"It'll grow out."

"Mom's going to be furious." The cat's cries finally got the girl's attention. "What's the matter with Boo Boo?"

"He hates riding in the car."

They parked in front of the clinic and hauled the kennel inside. In the reception room, Boo Boo spat and hissed fiercely. Connie sat in front of the cage and talked quietly. She stuck a finger through the bars and stroked him with it, until he bit her. "Ow! You little shit."

Jo looked her way and put a finger to her lips. "Not here," she warned.

Dr. Bender chose that moment to emerge from one of the examining rooms. "Bring him in. I'll take a look at him."

Connie lugged the kennel while Jo followed.

Laura Bender dumped the cat onto the examining table. She looked at his front feet, which he jerked away, and glanced under his tail at the small, empty sack. Then she stroked him. "Some feel cornered in a kennel, some feel safe. I'm going to give him a little shot to calm him down."

The cat collapsed in a heap of hair, the meows temporarily silenced.

Jo told her how she and Connie collaborated to keep the animal's origins from Connie's mother.

"Well, whatever works. At least Boo Boo here has a new home. I'll bet he likes being warm and safe and well fed."

"He bit me," Connie said, holding up her finger.

"He was stressed," the vet said with a small smile. "He really did a number on your aunt's hand last time he was here."

Connie looked taken back. "She's not my aunt," she said, glancing at Jo.

"Your friend in need, then," Laura added.

"My mother's friend," Connie corrected with another baleful look.

Jo knew she should have known better than to expect a change of heart. But the rejection hurt.

The cat was hustled back into the kennel. Connie carried it to the reception area.

With a shrug and lifted brows, Jo met Laura Bender's gray gaze. "I guess I tried to win her over with the cat."

The vet looked into her eyes. Jo thought she saw understanding dawn. She gave a nod.

"Thanks. I'll go pay the bill."

"No charge for a post surgery exam," Dr. Bender said.

Jo backed out of the room. "Thanks again," she added, trying to think of something else to say. But nothing came to mind.

IX

Connie got into the back seat with the cat, which immediately resumed its yowling. Jo threw an annoyed glance at the two of them.

"I feel like a chauffeur."

"Maybe he won't be so scared if I'm back here with him," the girl said. "Don't tell Mom about my hair, okay?"

Jo stifled a laugh. "You don't think she's going to notice?"

"I'll put on a hat."

"Good idea," she said sarcastically and pulled out of the parking lot with a screech of tires.

"Jeez, don't kill us," Connie said. "Could we maybe get some dye at Shopko or someplace?"

Jo glanced at Connie in the rearview mirror. "You know, you treat me like shit and then expect me to help you out."

"Okay, forget it," the girl said sullenly. "You'll be responsible for my death."

Jo laughed loudly. "All right. You win. But Boo's not going to like being left in the car."

"He'll live," the girl said, "won't you, Boo?"

Inside Shopko, she and Connie mulled over the many hair colors. Connie settled for a dark brown.

"Think it'll be close enough to fool Mom?" Connie asked.

"I don't think you should try to fool your mom," she said. "Tell her. She'll be okay with it."

Connie snorted her disbelief. "Are you out of your mind?"

On the drive home she glanced in the rearview mirror and saw the girl had tucked her hair under a ball cap. Connie was reading the back of the dye box.

Jo carried the cat into the house. Connie jumped out of the car and disappeared inside. The downstairs felt empty with only the clock ticking and the refrigerator humming. Gail was gone, she guessed, probably shopping. No radio, just Connie clomping around upstairs. The girl had lucked out. Released from its cage, the cat stopped its mewling.

Climbing the stairs, she knocked on the closed bathroom door. "Need any help?" she called.

"Keep Mom away, will you?"

"I'll be leaving soon." She went down to the kitchen and phoned Kim.

"Ready? I'm going to pick up the truck. Want to meet me at Mark's?" She didn't own enough furniture to fill a truck, but there was no hitch on the Chrysler or Kim's car. "Is Brad coming?"

"He had another meeting with the people fighting the factory farm this morning."

"It's okay, Kim."

"It's true, though. He'll help unload. I'm going to bring

Max and Lauren. They can carry small things. I'll leave the little ones with the neighbors."

"See you there."

When she pulled up in front of the house, a shower of yellow leaves fell from the huge maple next to the driveway. With arms crossed over a flannel shirt, Kim waited on the front porch with Mark. She heard the kids' voices down by the pool. Mark looked thin and angry. The last of her belongings would be taken from the house today. She'd be gone.

She rolled the back door of the U-Haul up with difficulty. "Hi, Kim. Hello, Mark," she said.

Mark turned his back and led the way inside. As they followed, she threw her sister a questioning look and whispered, "He's mad, right?"

"He's upset. It's understandable, don't you think?"

Mark disappeared into the backyard and sent Lauren and Max inside. Through a window she saw him skimming fallen leaves off the pool, the sunlight glinting on his dark hair.

An hour and a half later they had the furniture loaded. She went around the house to the pool. The sun was warm on her face, and she shaded her eyes from the glare. "We're leaving," she called to Mark, who was cleaning out the filter, then added, "Almost time to drain it."

He grunted something without looking up.

She followed the Audi through the leaf cluttered streets. The rain the day before had brought them to the ground where they lay curled and darkening. Backing into Kim's driveway, she jumped out.

The garage door went up and Brad walked through the opening, pulling on gloves. He flexed his arms and shoulders, and she smiled a little. Brad had grown a paunch in the past few years and was going bald, but was still a good looking man. What hair he had was curly. His eyes were the soft brown of a cocker spaniel's.

The twins darted across the yard from the neighboring

house. She hugged them and then forgot them. As she and Brad lugged a mattress through the garage, the truck started rolling slowly toward the street. For a second, Jo stared in disbelief. They dropped the mattress and ran.

"Jesus Christ," Brad yelled, sprinting toward the cab of the truck with her dashing after.

The truck hit the back of a pickup parked in the driveway across the street and jolted to a stop. Jo's heart jumped around inside her chest like it had broken loose.

The twins were perched on the front seat of the U-Haul, their eyes big and frightened. She would have laughed had she been able to stop shaking.

Brad climbed inside, backed the truck into his driveway. He turned off the engine and set the parking brake, which she hadn't done. No one was hurt, not even the pickup. A Reese hitch protected its steel bumper.

Kim grabbed the twins out of the truck and sent them inside. "Go to your rooms. Now," she said.

"It's my fault, Kimmie. I'm so sorry. I might have killed them," Jo said, feeling ill.

"They know better. We can't watch them every minute."

"Come on, Jo," Brad said, picking up his end of the mattress while Kim held the door to the house open.

Late in the afternoon, Jo pulled under the overhang and sat in the Sebring until Gail came outside. Every muscle ached. She'd developed a headache when the twins put the truck in neutral and rolled out of the driveway. It nagged at the back of her skull.

Gail opened the passenger door and peered in at her. "Why are you sitting out here?"

"I'm tired. I've been on the go all day. How was your day?"

"Okay. Where did Connie go? Do you know?"

She shook her head. She'd hoped she wouldn't be around when Gail glimpsed Connie's dye job. If it looked anything like the earlier one, it would be god-awful.

"She'll show up," she said, getting out. The day was still

warm. It smelled of fall, a dusty odor that hung in the air. "Nice out. Want to sit on the patio?"

French doors opened onto the small cement slab outside the dining room. Bird feeders hung from shepherds' crooks around the perimeter of concrete. A glass topped wrought iron table with four chairs took up most of the paved surface.

Jo told Gail about her day, leaving out Connie's hair.

"Do you know a Laura Bender?" she asked. "She's the vet."

"Why would I know her?"

Jo shrugged a little. Dust motes danced in the last rays of sunlight. She felt herself relaxing, her muscles relinquishing their grip, her headache dissolving. "I thought I felt vibes." What Gail called gay radar.

Gail smiled slightly. "You always feel vibes."

Hearing the kitchen door open, Jo tensed. Connie must be home.

Gail called for her daughter to join them.

When Connie stood inside the open French doors, looking out at them through the screen, it was impossible to see anything different about her.

"Come on out," Gail urged.

Connie stepped hesitantly onto the patio. Her hair looked too dark to be her own, but Jo thought maybe that was because she was so aware that it had been dyed and redyed.

Gail put an arm around her daughter's waist and Connie leaned into her mother's chair. Jo saw the yearning in the girl's face and wondered about it. Then the girl straightened, squared her shoulders, and moved away.

At dinner, under the dangling overhead light, Gail studied her daughter with a bewildered frown. "Your hair looks different, Connie. It's so dark."

"Looks the same to me," Jo said. It was more than a shade darker and shone dully under the glare.

"I tried a rinse on it last night."

"You dyed it?" Gail asked.

"We all did, Mom, and I hate it." With a wail, Connie jumped up from her chair, upsetting it, and ran upstairs.

"Well, at least it's not blond or red," Gail said resignedly.

Jo laughed, choking on the food she was swallowing.

Connie was locked in the upstairs bathroom the next morning. "I gotta go," Jo said, knocking on the door.

The girl flung it open. Her hair stood out around her head like brown straw. "Look at it," the girl said, grabbing a hunk. "I can't do anything with it."

Without thinking, Jo reached out and touched the dry strands. They felt like they looked. "Conditioner, lots of it," she counseled, "but first let me use the john."

Gail wanted to exercise at the Y and eat breakfast out afterwards. They'd met at the Y on the exercise machines. Smiling, she remembered how they had begun to talk, how the talk had led to coffee afterwards, how the coffee had led to an occasional movie. Somewhere along the way, she'd gone home with Gail when Connie was at her dad's and they'd ended up in bed.

Connie was waiting to go back in when Jo came out of the bathroom. "You want to go to the Y with us? Breakfast out afterwards."

The girl was already shaking her head. "I'm going to Mimi's when she gets home from church."

"How come I've never met her?" Jo asked as Connie started to close the door.

"Get serious," the girl said. "What would I tell her? There are only two bedrooms. She's not stupid."

She thought about Connie's remarks later as the hot spray drifted over her in the Y shower cubicle. She hadn't wondered why Connie never brought friends home. It made her feel bad to know she was the reason. Maybe she and Gail were selfish to foist their relationship onto the girl. At any rate, this living together held very little romance. Not enough to make it worthwhile. She could see Gail when Connie was at her dad's.

Over breakfast she brought this up. "Maybe I shouldn't have moved in."

"She'll learn to love you," Gail said.

She responded as Connie might have. "Get real."

X

Looking out the window at leaves scuttling before a cold November wind, Jo almost wished herself at her mother's condo in Florida. Although she found Florida's flat terrain, scrubby brush and runaway development unappealing, she liked the perpetual summer, the wildlife, and the ocean.

Her mother was urging her to come for a visit in December. "You and Kimberly almost never come to see me."

"Yes, we do," she countered, remembering the condominiums wrapped around a golf course where her mother and stepfather spent their mornings.

"Once a year for a few days."

"I'll talk to Kim, but I doubt if she can get away. The older kids are in school." Had their mother met all of her grandchildren? She had returned for a visit once or twice, but it had been years. Kim never took the children with her when she went.

"Kim suggested I come there. This time of year. Can you imagine?"

"You'd hate it," she said, fervently hoping she wouldn't.

A silence followed while Jo stared out the window, anticipating the bite of the ferocious wind with a shiver. She detested November. Cold, gray weather without the beauty of snow.

"I'll talk to Stan about it. He's golfing right now. It's seventy-five degrees, too hot for me."

Envious, Jo said, "Maybe in February or March I can come over a long weekend." That was when she really needed a break from winter. Walter would tell her to go, enjoy herself. He'd pick up her work without complaint.

Her mother broke into an unstoppable cough, which seemed the way they ended conversations these days, and hung up. Jo phoned Kim in a panic.

"I just spoke to Mother. She talked like she might actually consider a visit. She can't stay with me, Kim. What would I tell her?" She thought of Connie unwilling to bring her friends home and understood.

"Whoa, girl," Kim replied. "Calm down. We'll put the little girls in together. That'll free up a bedroom here."

"Why is she thinking about coming now?"

"She hasn't met the twins or Sydney, but I don't think that's why, much as I'd like to. I think she's feeling mortal."

"I thought she was going to choke on the stuff in her throat," Jo said, her mood turning as gloomy as the day.

Gail sat next to Jo, wrapped warm arms around her, and silently rocked her.

"I'll talk to you next week sometime," she said to Kim, ending the conversation.

Turning, she enclosed Gail in an embrace and pulled her

down on top of her. They had made love before getting up that morning, so the rush of passion as she brushed her lips over Gail's face and neck was unexpected.

She went right to the source, fearing Gail would change her mind, knowing she had to get her past the point of no return quickly. Then, tucked intimately between Gail's legs, she found herself listening for a key in the lock. What if Connie came home from her dad's to get her homework or something and found them in this position? The girl would never forgive her. She might be seriously traumatized.

Lifting her head, she said, "Let's go to bed."

They pulled their clothes together and climbed the stairs, but between the living room and the bedroom, some of the desire disappeared. Achieving orgasm became something of a chore.

Afterwards, Gail slept while Jo curled against her and listened to the wind. She must have fallen asleep, too, because she awoke to an empty bed.

The peaceful weekend ended when Connie came home late Sunday afternoon, argumentative and crabby. "What's wrong?" Gail asked when she saw her daughter's face.

Jo could have told Gail it was a mistake to comment. She recalled her own mother telling her to "Wipe that look off your face," when she hadn't even said anything.

"Nothing." Connie snapped, then lifted the cat gently. "I'm going upstairs."

Connie appeared once while Jo and Gail were watching Bramwell on Masterpiece Theater. She fixed herself a peanut butter sandwich, filled a bowl with the popcorn Gail had made, and clomped upstairs to her room.

Gail seemed only mildy curious about what had gone wrong with Connie's visit with her dad. Jo speculated from past observations that Gail gained some measure of reassurance when things appeared to go awry between Connie and her dad.

She moved closer till her hip touched Gail's.

* * * * *

Keith Cyszka was sitting in the waiting room when she stopped at the reception desk Monday morning. He was the guy who wanted a temporary driving job. He had been there every workday since the interview. Maybe he thought his presence would spur her into finding him work.

Carol followed her into her office and closed the door. "This guy is driving me nuts. He even asked me out."

"Tell him I'll call when I find something for him. That he should go home and wait."

"I have," Carol said. "It does no good. He doesn't listen."

"Send him in." She sighed.

"I like coming here," he said, smiling, showing gaps between his molars.

"Go to the library, look for a job, do anything else, but don't come here unless we ask you to," she said, "and when I find something for you, I want you to shave and put on clean clothes."

"Hey lady, who do you think you are?" The smile was gone, his tone threatening.

"Take my advice if you want to be my client." She paused. "Do you understand?"

"You can't tell me what to do," he huffed.

"I can ask you not to disrupt our days. We'll call when there's a job for you."

He got up abruptly and left, banging the door.

Carol stuck her head in the door. "He's gone. Thanks."

She was shaking. Confrontation was not her thing. Walter came in with coffee for their daily meeting.

"I'll take care of him if he comes back," he promised.

The night was dark and cold and still when she walked to her car in the mostly empty parking lot. Locking the door behind her, she started the engine. Earlier she had called Gail from work and left a message on the machine that she would be late.

Gail hurried into the kitchen when Jo came through the side door, filling her with the oddest dread. Voices murmured in the living room from the TV.

"Kim has phoned three times." Gail handed her the portable phone.

"Kim? It's me," she said quietly into the receiver.

"Mom had a stroke. Stan called to say she's in a hospital in Cocoa. He said not to call, that he'd keep us up to date."

Jo was already making mental notes: Call Walter, make reservations, pack, withdraw money from the ATM machine. "Go with me," she said.

"Let's overlap. That way we'll stretch out the visit. You can pick me up at Orlando in four days. By then I'll have made arrangements for the kids. Do you need a ride to the airport?"

"Probably. I'll call you back." She hung up and went into the living room where Gail was watching a program on Ella Fitzgerald.

Gail took her hand, pulled her next to her on the sofa, and put a sympathetic arm around her. She leaned into it.

"I knew it," she said later, sitting on the bed while Gail helped her pack. "I always thought there'd be time to make things right with my mother."

"There's still time," Gail reassured her.

Kim dropped her off at the airport the next morning. It took both of them to lift her suitcase out of the back of the Audi. She'd packed everything she could think of, including appropriate dress clothes for a funeral — just in case.

Rolling the luggage across the smooth floor, she looked up and was surprised to see Laura Bender talking to a man while waiting to check in at the Delta counter. She got in line behind them.

Sure that the man was Laura's husband, she learned that

he was her brother seeing Laura off. Jo waited a discreet distance while they said good-bye, then walked to the waiting plane with Laura. Laura said she was going to Florida to visit a friend from vet school. Their seats were not together. The plane was filled with business people.

When they disembarked at the Orlando airport, Laura handed her a card with her friend's number on it. "Call if you get a chance. Let me know how your mother is."

Jo's stepfather met her at the luggage carousel after everyone else had grabbed their baggage and left. She was beginning to feel abandoned when she saw him coming her way. Tall and stooped and so thin his neck was birdlike, Stan hefted her suitcase as if he were a much younger man. Pecking her on the cheek, he smiled, showing false teeth.

"How's Mother?" she asked.

"You'll see," he replied. On the drive to Cocoa he remained close-mouthed. And when they rolled into the garage, he said, "This was her idea, not mine."

She had been wondering why they weren't going to the hospital, and asked.

"Because she's not in the hospital." He hauled her suitcase out of the trunk and dragged it inside. "See for yourself."

Her mother was sitting on a white leather couch, looking amazingly well. "Surprise!" she said, smiling shakily.

Jo looked from her white haired mother to Stan. "What's going on?"

"This was the only way I could think of getting you here," her mother said brightly.

"You lied?" she asked in disbelief. "You never had a stroke?"

"No, I did have a stroke. A little, bitty one, didn't I, Stan?"

"Yes, you did, Ginger."

Jo stared at her mother. "When?" was all she could think to say.

"A week ago, after talking to Kim. A blood vessel broke in my head."

"From coughing?" She watched her mother light up, her long, elegant fingers yellowed. "Put that cigarette out," she said angrily. "I'm not breathing secondhand smoke."

"Don't tell Kim," her mother begged, standing up and crossing the tiled floor, her slim figure stiffly upright. As she closed the distance between them, Jo noticed the taut cords in her neck, the deep lines on her face. Her mother resembled a piece of beef jerky, sun dried and tough.

XI

Jo called neither Kim nor Gail. If she talked to either one, she would tell them. She hardly believed that she was going to let this hoax continue. Maybe she and Kim deserved it. It had taken a phony stroke to bring her here. Kim should have brought her kids to meet their grandmother years ago. Why did she and her sister expect their mother to come to them?

And right behind these thoughts, nagging to come to the surface, was the fact that Laura Bender was not far away. She itched to call her, to hear her voice, to tell someone what had happened.

She sneaked down the hall into the den. The house was so quiet it unnerved her. Closing the door behind her, she sat down on another white couch, this one covered in cloth, and pushed in the digits on the card Laura had given her. It was ten o'clock. Her mother and Stan were in bed.

"Hi," she whispered, when a woman answered. "Is Laura there?"

"Yes, she is," the woman said and put Laura on.

"It's Jo," she said nervously.

"How's your mother?" Laura asked with concern.

"She faked the stroke," she said in hushed tones. "She's home and real perky." A small silence followed.

"Why do you think she did that?"

Jo shrugged to herself. "To get me and my sister here."

"Well, it got you here."

"Kim will arrive in four days if I don't tell her."

"Are you going to?"

"No."

"Look. My friend has to work, but I'm going to the Canaveral National Seashore day after tomorrow. Would you like to meet in the park building? Are you a birder?"

"I don't know if you'd call me a birder. I don't feel a need to identify every flying object I see."

Laura's laugh floated over the line, making Jo smile. "Well, I am a hardcore birder. If you can put up with that, I'll be at the building between nine and ten in the morning."

"Isn't that kind of late for birding? I thought dawn was nearly too late."

Another laugh. "Yes, but I added time in case I lose my way."

Jo crept toward her room on bare feet cooled by the tile floors. The condo was a one story Spanish style with a stucco exterior, cream colored plaster interior walls, and ceramic floors. There was a small patio enclosed by the condo's interior walls that she passed in the hallway. She stepped outside into the warm thickly humid night. It smelled of something blooming. Sitting in one of the lounge chairs, she fell asleep.

Her mother found her there the next morning. "I thought you'd gone back home when you weren't in your bed."

Jo felt momentarily disorientated. She glanced at the blue sky, visible directly above. "What's on the agenda for today?"

"What would you like to do?" her mother asked, setting two cups of coffee on the glass topped wrought iron table.

She couldn't remember her mother ever asking her what she wanted. Surely she had. "Go to the beach, enjoy the sun." She asked, "Don't you always golf in the morning?"

"You don't golf nor do you visit every day. I don't want to go off and leave you. I can't be in the sun long, though. I break out in hives. It really is hot down here." Her mother's skin attested to the effects of too much sun.

"Are you okay, Mom? Do you feel all right?" she asked as her mother lit up a cigarette and broke into a ragged cough. "I wish you wouldn't smoke. That stroke was a warning."

"I tried to stop. I was too stressed," her mother managed to say between hacks. Her eyes, big and brown, dominated her face.

"Did you try the patches?" she persisted.

"Yes, I did." Her mother had gotten the cough under control. She wrapped her robe tightly around herself and rasped, "You and your sister never smoked, so you don't understand."

Jo acceded. She could thank her mother's example for that. Early on, she had learned to hate the smoke, the smell, the cigarette butts everywhere. "I guess that's true. Are you cold? We can go inside."

"I'm fine. We'll go for a drive. Stan's leaving soon; he golfs every morning unless it pours. I confess I am glad for a break. Even golf gets boring if you do it day in and day out." She took a deep breath of smoke and coughed it out.

In the car, heading across the causeway, her mother asked if she was living with someone. Jo considered giving an honest answer, then decided her mother really didn't want the unvarnished truth. She said she'd moved in with a friend and her daughter.

The brown eyes scanned Jo's face. "You always had lots of girl friends, so many that I worried about your lack of interest in boys. I'd like to have one good woman friend, someone to confide in."

"What do you want to confide?" Jo asked, wary of an answer.

"Nothing terribly serious. I have bridge playing friends, golfing friends. It's a good life down here."

She feared her mother was dying and knew it, but if her mother wasn't willing to tell . . . "I'm meeting a friend at the Canaveral National Seashore tomorrow morning. Would you like to come?"

"Thanks, but no thanks. You can drive my car, though. We'll do something when you get back in the afternoon. Do you still play bridge?"

"I haven't played in years. I don't know if you'd want to be my partner."

When they parked along the shore of the intracoastal waterway, Jo came upon a few hardshelled creatures with tiny tails in the shallow water. They looked like hinged turtles to her without heads and legs. She hauled one to the car for her mother to identify.

"Horseshoe crab," her mother said. "Put it back where it belongs. Nasty looking thing. It's kind of late for them to be mating."

Her mother treated her to lunch at an upscale restaurant. While Jo devoured fresh seafood as if it might scuttle off, her mother took only a few bites before pushing the plate away. Lighting a cigarette, her mother drank the glass of wine she'd ordered.

"No wonder you're so thin, Mother. Is this how you always eat?" Bright sunlight streamed in through tall windows. "I'll finish it." But when she reached for the plate, her mother lightly slapped her hand.

"If you want more, we'll order more." She broke into a

cough that must have hurt. “It’s rude to eat off someone else’s plate.”

“I hate waste,” Jo said, “and it’s no more rude that coughing your guts out over a cigarette.”

Her mother glared but did not snuff out the cigarette. “Finish your meal,” she said when she could talk again. “We’ll go home then.”

Jo had overstepped her bounds. She nodded. “We should call Kim anyway.” The only person she’d phoned since arriving was Laura. Tonight she’d call Gail.

Her mother parked herself within listening range while she talked to Kim. “I’m here, the weather’s wonderful, Mother’s home.”

“Already? How is she?” Kim asked.

Jo glanced at their mother, who sat on the white sofa a few feet away, “Talk to her yourself,” and handed the phone over.

Determined to enjoy the warm weather while there, she took a book outside to the swimming pool and clubhouse that served the condominium.

The next day she crossed the causeway to Merritt Island and made her way north to the Canaveral National Seashore, both eager and anxious.

Later, as she and Laura walked along the relatively deserted beach, stopping to squint at dolphins surfacing in the distance, amused by the comical sight of pelicans folding their wings and diving headfirst into the water, picking up shells left by the retreating tide, Jo found herself at a loss for conversation. Laura seemed to feel no need to talk.

At one point Laura shaded her eyes with a hand and scanned the water. “I love the ocean. You see more wildlife on the intracoastal waterway, though.”

"Should we go there?" Jo asked.

"When you're ready," Laura replied.

"I'm ready," Jo said, although she much preferred the ocean side. "Who's taking care of your dog?"

"He's at the clinic. They give him the run of the place."

"I'd prefer a dog, but he'd be alone all day during the week. Boo Boo doesn't seem to mind." They headed back toward the parking lot where they'd left their cars.

"That's why cats are the more popular pets. You were kind to take on Boo Boo's case."

"I wasn't being kind. I was trying to get Connie to see me as an ally. I lied to her mother." She felt her shoes filling up with sand that bunched under her arches.

"White lies, I'm sure." Laura smiled.

"Well, it didn't work." She told Laura of the hair dying incident and smiled when Laura laughed. "That didn't work either."

"Keep trying. Something will."

"I don't know why I care. Do you have children?"

"Nope. Never married."

"I don't have children either, but I had a great stepson."

Laura threw her a look, her face flushed from the sun. "I thought you lived with Connie and her mother."

"I do. I'm getting a divorce." She had yet to call Audrey Compton. "Do you live by yourself?"

"Yep." They slogged on through the sand, the wind off the ocean jerking at their hair and clothes.

"What do you do for fun besides birding?"

"I read, cross country ski, hike. What about you?"

"The same," she said, although she hadn't been doing much of anything lately except work. "I'm just settling into a new routine."

They reached the parking lot, where they took Jo's car.

"Actually, my life is pretty much structured around work and the dog," Laura said.

"I see," Jo said, although she only saw bits and pieces. She longed to fill in the blanks. She was convinced Laura's life was more interesting than her own.

When they crossed over to the intracoastal waterway, they saw ospreys, herons, egrets. All their talk turned to birds until she drove Laura back to her vehicle.

Before getting into her car, Laura said, "It's always more fun birding with someone else. Thanks for meeting me."

"Thank you," she replied. "What are your plans the rest of the week?"

"My friend's taken time off. We're going to the Everglades for a few days."

"Sounds like fun. See you up north." She couldn't very well ask to go along. It would be too rude. How could she go off and leave her mother anyway even if Laura invited her? Which she hadn't.

On the drive back to her mother's home, Jo wondered what she had thought or hoped would happen. It had been an innocent meeting. Yet in her imagination it had held dangerous possibilities. She hadn't told Gail when she'd talked to her. She probably never would.

Feeling let down, she parked in the garage and entered the cool interior of her mother's home. She'd hoped for more, some insight into Laura's life, an invitation to become a part of it. She had left knowing little more about Laura than that she had a dog, she lived alone, and she enjoyed certain hobbies.

She found her mother and stepfather playing bridge with another couple. Her mother smiled at her. "Hi, darling, how was the birding?"

"Great."

"Let me introduce our friends."

As soon as politely possible, she escaped to the swimming pool with a book.

* * * * *

When she spied Kim at the airport, Jo felt relieved. She hugged her sister as if she hadn't seen her in weeks. "You're a welcome breath of home."

"Are you all alone?"

"Yep. Stan is golfing. Mother's at the condo, of course. You're in for a surprise, though."

"Come on. Tell me. Give me a hint at least," Kim said, as they put her bag on a luggage cart and walked to the car.

Jo slammed the trunk lid and turned to her sister. "Let's hit the road."

"No fair. What's the surprise?"

"I'll tell you once we're on the highway. I have to concentrate on traffic."

As they sped toward Cocoa, Jo threw a look at Kim. "Mom's all right."

"That's the surprise?" Kim asked.

"She didn't have a stroke. Well, she did have a small one a week before Stan called." A Cadillac lurched into their lane, nearly clipping their bumper. Jo swore and hit the horn. The close call reminded her of her accident with Mark and left her with weak legs and an overload of adrenaline. "These old farts are dangerous drivers."

When Kim failed to laugh, she chanced another glance at her. Kim said, "Do you know how hard it was for me to get away?"

"It was for me too. I had to drop everything in Walter's lap."

"Why didn't you tell me? I would have cancelled." Kim's angry gaze fixed on Jo. "Some surprise."

"I was angry too when I walked in the door and saw Mother looking so well. But should she have to pretend a stroke to get us to visit her? Would you have come otherwise? I wouldn't have, not now anyway."

Kim gazed out the passenger window and sighed loudly. She unrolled the glass and warm air whipped into the vehicle.

"Feel that? It was in the forties when I left home with a wind that ripped right through clothes."

"What are you getting at?" Jo asked.

"Now that I'm here I think I'll try to enjoy it." After a short silence, Kim continued, "Should we be ashamed, considering Mother's history as a parent?"

"I don't know. I'm still sorting that out." She'd never felt valued in her mother's eyes. "She's different. She even asked what I wanted to do."

"Do you think she's trying to make amends? I've always believed she'd have liked us better had we been boys."

"I always wanted to be a boy." Jo grinned.

"That figures," Kim said dryly.

XII

While sitting on the deck of a restaurant that evening as a riot of colors stained the sky and water, a vivid image of Laura's sun-rosy face silenced Jo in midsentence.

"What, Jo?" Kim asked.

But she'd forgotten what she'd been saying.

Her mother's husky voice lamented. "You girls were always so secretive about everything. Why couldn't you share?"

She met Kim's eyes. They'd been close-mouthed, it was true. Their mother had been so critical. Jo remembered feeling crushed by her disapproval. "You could have been more supportive, Mother."

"Not when I didn't know what I was supposed to support." Their mother blew a long stream of smoke over their heads.

"I don't know why you have to bring up the past. Let it go," Stan said, flagging the waitress for more drinks.

When they returned to the condo, Jo felt lightheaded. Her mother and Stan were not only heavy smokers, they were hard drinkers. She and Kim could not keep up with them.

Stan called her to the phone when she and Kim were getting ready for bed. "It's probably Gail," she said, grabbing a robe.

"I apologize. I don't normally phone anyone this late," Laura said.

"How are the Everglades?" Jo asked, more surprised than anything.

"We didn't go. There was an emergency at the clinic. Did you read about it? One of those puppy farms was closed down, and we were inundated with sick animals. I've been working."

"That doesn't sound like fun," she said.

"How are things going there?"

"My sister, Kim, arrived today. We all went out to eat tonight."

"Does your mom want a puppy? Do you?" Laura laughed. "Just kidding. It was on the news last night and people have been calling in to adopt all day. It's madness."

"I'm supposed to go home on Sunday," she said. This was Thursday.

"Me too," Laura said. "That's why I called. I thought maybe we could spend Saturday night in Orlando. I have a morning flight."

Stunned, Jo felt her face flush. It sounded like a come-on to her. She hesitated only a moment. It made sense. "I'm flying out in the morning too, probably on the same plane as you are. Where are you staying?"

"I've made a reservation at the Hilton. I could only get

one room, but it has two double beds. Do you mind sharing? I don't think I snore." Laura laughed again.

Shaken, Jo stammered, "I don't either as far as I know."

The next morning when Stan left to golf, Jo, Kim, and their mother took their coffee to the small inner patio. "I think it's time to have a heart-to-heart," their mother said.

Jo saw her own alarm mirrored in Kim's eyes. "About what?" she ventured. She could not recall the three of them having a serious discussion together.

"About why I connived to get you here." Their mother shook a cigarette out of the pack in the pocket of her robe. She lit it, inhaled deeply, and aimed the smoke at the cube of sky.

"You are ill, aren't you, Mother?" Kim asked.

"Let's say, I've had a few warnings." Their mother shot looks at one then the other before continuing. "Don't interrupt. Look, I know I wasn't the best mother in the world. I tried, though. You two shut me out. You still do." Lifting a hand at Jo and Kim's polite murmurs of denial, she went on. "It's okay. But now I want us to be closer." She blew a new stream of smoke into the air where it mingled with the others and hung above their heads. "By the way, you'll each get a third of my estate."

"Mom," Kim complained, "what a guilt trip."

Their mother shrugged and lifted one thin eyebrow. "That's what mothers do best — instill guilt. It's how we make you behave." She turned to Jo. "Now tell me the truth. Was Mark cheating on you?"

Taken aback, Jo said, "No."

"Then why did you leave him?"

"Does that have to be the only reason to leave?"

"Don't answer a question with a question."

"All right," she said. "You want to know the truth, I was cheating on him."

Her mother fought back a smile. "You found a better man than Mark. Tell me about him."

"I found a woman." She held her breath.

Her mother pinned her with a fierce look. "Just like your father."

"What does he have to do with it?"

"He was a pervert. He must have influenced you." Her mother's dismay poured out of her huge brown eyes. "It wasn't anything I did. I'm not that way."

"You mean he was gay?" Kim asked.

"I think I was always this way," Jo said. "I just didn't know it."

"People aren't born homosexual," her mother said scornfully.

"It's not something you catch, like the flu," Kim put in.

"Where'd she get such an idea?" their mother scoffed.

"There's scientific proof, Mom. Don't you read the newspapers?" Kim persisted.

"She can't have my genes."

"Don't talk about me like I'm not here." Jo shook with rage. "And don't ask for the truth if you don't want to hear it." She stumbled inside to dress.

Kim followed a few minutes later. "Why did you tell her?" she asked as Jo jerked on shorts and a T-shirt.

"Beause I misjudged her. Again. I should know better. She never fails to disappoint me." She wiped away tears with her hand and shirt. "And I never fail to disappoint her."

"Where are you going?"

"Out."

"Can I come with?"

"Get some clothes on then."

Jo quietly steamed as they walked along the curbs that wound through condominium and trailer complexes.

"All these years I hid in the closet because of her. She'll never get it."

"I can't get over our father being a gay man. Maybe it is hereditary. I can't even remember him. Can you?"

"No. She kept him away. I hate her."

"But you don't, Jo. That's the problem. Just like me, you're still trying to woo her."

"How can I go back there after this?"

"Only one more day after today. You can do it. Maybe I should fly home with you."

"No, Kim," she said a little too forcefully. "Stay till Tuesday like you said you would. You can drive me to Orlando Saturday afternoon. We'll go early. I'm meeting a friend."

Kim leaned over and peered in her face. "Do I know this friend?"

"I don't know. Maybe." She tried to sound casual. "Dr. Laura Bender. She's the veterinarian at the clinic where I took the cat. Do you know her?"

"Yeah, I do. I've used her in emergencies. I didn't realize she was a friend of yours."

"Well, she's not really. We flew down together; we're flying back on the same plane. It leaves Sunday morning. It makes sense to stay overnight."

"I guess." Kim shrugged. "Did you tell Gail?"

"No." She blushed.

"There's something going on here, isn't there?" Kim persisted.

"No." She stopped walking and looked around. "Let's find some place to get a cup of coffee."

"You want me to mind my own business?" Kim asked as she stirred sugar into her coffee.

"Yes, I do."

"I'll bet you never knew I cheated on Brad last year." Kim said in a conversational tone.

Her mouth dropped open. "No, I didn't. Why'd you do that and with whom?"

"Someone I knew from college. Remember, Brad didn't go with me to my high school reunion? I understood when you cheated on Mark, but you haven't been with Gail long enough to need a little fling."

"Who said I was going to cheat? It's the last thing on my mind."

Kim gave her a serious stare. "You can tell me anything, Jo, and I won't repeat it, but don't ever lie to me."

When they left the restaurant, neither could recall the route they'd taken to get there. The sun beat down out of a cloudless sky. No one else was walking the streets. They both cried out in relief when Stan's Jeep pulled up next to them.

"Get in," he said. "Your mother's home crying nonstop. What did you say to her?" he asked.

Uncaring, Jo said, "I told her I was a lesbian."

In the pause that followed she heard Kim's small nervous giggle and Stan's heavy breathing. "Well, that would do it. I don't know what she said to you, but ignore it. She spouts off at the mouth and says things she doesn't mean when you tell her something she doesn't want to hear." He was looking at them in the rearview mirror. "Your old man was gay. Did she tell you that? She took it as a personal insult."

"Yep. She told us," Kim said.

He dropped them off in front of the condo before continuing on to the country club. "She'll be nice to you now," he said. "Just forget what she said before. That's what I do."

They took Stan's advice. It worked. Their mother behaved as if there'd been no angry words exchanged. She took them shopping, insisted on buying them each an outfit to wear out to dinner at the clubhouse that night, then drove them for lunch to a seafood restaurant near the market where fishermen sold their catch.

Jo caught her mother's puzzled gaze on her. "What?" she finally said.

"I should have known. You and your girl friends were too tight."

Nervously, Jo laughed. "I didn't know back then."

"Your father was an embarrassment. I had to go to court to keep him from seeing you. When I married Stan, though, he stopped trying."

"What was his name?" Kim asked.

"Joe Stanford. You look like him, Jo." She snorted a laugh. "You are like him."

That's why her mother had a hard time with her. "Guess so."

"Oh, come on." Her mother gave her a friendly slap on the forearm as if everything were forgiven. "Let's go show Kim those nasty horseshoe crabs."

"Do you think we can find him?" Kim asked later. The arthropods were gone.

"Our father?" It seemed odd to hear that word in reference to themselves. Fathers had belonged to other kids. She'd never thought of Stan as a father. He'd been more like a live-in friend of the family.

"Maybe he's still around."

"Maybe," she said. "I'll look in the phone book when I get home." Tomorrow she'd be in Orlando with Laura. Her heart lost some of its heaviness.

She and Kim left for Orlando after lunch on Saturday. Stan loaded her bag in the back of the car, while she said good-bye to her mother.

"Take care of yourself, dear. Practice safe sex, will you?"

Poised to kiss her mother on the cheek, instead she searched the brown eyes for humor.

"Mother, lesbians are the least likely population segment to contract HIV," Kim said.

"Oh. I suppose you're going to look for your father."

"Don't say it, Mom," Jo warned.

"I'm just worried about you. You are my daughters."

Jo bit her tongue. She didn't want to part in anger. "You take care, Mother. It's your turn to visit."

Stan waved from the driveway, their mother stood at the front door. As Kim stepped on the accelerater and drove them away, Jo let out her breath. "Do you believe those last remarks? Sometimes I could strangle her."

"Sometimes I think we should. She, who's supposed to be the guru of good manners, completely misses the point."

"What is the point?" Jo asked, a little lost.

"Isn't the essence of good manners to make the other person comfortable, mentally and physically?"

"I always thought good manners meant knowing which fork to use first."

"That too," Kim said, flashing a grin white against her sunburned skin.

"I like your definition better." She looked out the window at the speeding traffic. "How are we going to find him?"

"We could hire a private detective," Kim suggested. "Do you ever miss Mark?"

"Where did that come from?" Jo smiled. "Sometimes. I think in some ways it's easier to live with a man than a woman."

"I wouldn't have thought so. A woman helps with the cooking and cleaning and shares her feelings."

"A woman reads you better than a man. A man doesn't second guess. He takes you at your word. If you say nothing's wrong, he doesn't keep digging."

"Aha. What is wrong?"

Jo thought of how different real life with Gail was from how she had imagined it would be. "Maybe I expected too much."

"Didn't we all," Kim said wryly.

XIII

"Let me off out front, Kim. It's too much of a hassle to park." Together, they dragged the bag out of the trunk and stood for a moment under the hotel's protective canopy looking at each other. "I feel like a war survivor."

"You are, sweetie." Kim smoothed Jo's cheek with the back of her hand.

Jo leaned forward to kiss her. "Drive defensively. Thanks for the ride. See you at home."

A porter took her bag and put it on a luggage dolly, which she followed into the cool lobby. At the desk she learned that Laura had checked in. She rode in the elevator with the porter up to the fifth floor.

Knocking on the door, she was startled when it opened almost immediately. The porter carried the bag inside and closed the door as he left. Her smile quivered nervously.

"You're earlier than I thought you'd be," Laura said.

"My mother and I get along better from a distance." She felt a twist of guilt.

"My mother died two years ago. I'd give anything to have one more conversation with her." They were standing in the entryway.

"What would you say?"

"I'd tell her how much I admired her, and I'd ask her all the things I forgot to ask when she could answer."

Unexpected emotion clogged Jo's throat. She cleared it. "That's nice."

Laura backed into the room and sat on the end of one of the beds. "Is it okay if I take this one?"

"It doesn't matter." She threw her backpack on the other and flopped down next to it.

"Want to go out and explore a little?"

"Sure."

While investigating the nearby shops, they spent an hour at a bookstore where Jo bought a book for Gail and another for Connie. She had no idea what kind of books Connie read and asked the clerk for help.

"What are her interests?" the girl asked.

"She has a cat, if that helps."

The clerk suggested one of James Herriot's books.

On the way back to the hotel, they stopped at a Mexican restaurant. Sitting on a veranda, sipping margaritas and eating chips and salsa, Jo felt herself relaxing. "Did all the puppies get adopted?"

"Most of them. Calls were still coming in when I left. There were forty-three pups and ten mamas. It was a small backyard operation."

"What kind of dogs were they?"

"Daschunds. The mamas were in bad shape. The pups appeared to be in pretty good condition. They took the pups away as soon as possible so that the mothers could be rebred. The mamas were locked in small cages off the ground. They eliminated through the wire floors. Some could hardly walk, they'd been cooped up so long. Their paws were covered with sores."

It was more than Jo wanted to hear. "What will happen to the owners?"

"They'll be fined and lose their license."

"I suppose you see a lot of animal abuse," Jo said.

"I help out at the animal shelter. So, yes. People who are mistreating their pets don't take them to a veterinary clinic, though." Laura's clear gaze disconcerted Jo, who looked away. "I don't think you ever told me about your work."

"I work for a temporary job agency. There are two of us who do the placements, Walter and me."

"Walter must be missing you."

"I'm sure he is. He's a great guy," Jo said, studying the menu. "I think I'll have the enchilada dinner."

Darkness was falling when they left the restaurant. They said little as they walked back to the hotel. Jo fought sleep brought on by the margaritas and food and the week with her mother. She lay down on the bed.

Awakening alone in full darkness, she turned on a light and saw it was eight o'clock. Putting on her swimsuit, she grabbed a towel and went in search of the pool.

Laura sat between the pool and the whirlpool, reading a book she had purchased that afternoon. She wore a one piece knit black suit that showed cleavage. Jo felt desire stir as she dragged a chaise longue over.

"Are you feeling livelier now?" Laura asked.

"I'm sorry. I couldn't stay awake. Now I probably won't be able to go to sleep." Her gaze strayed to Laura's breasts, tucked together, moving up and down with every breath. "Maybe a swim will wake me up."

She counted twenty laps, then climbed out of the cool water and lowered herself into the spa. Laura joined her.

"Do you go to the Y?"

"Yeah. Are you a member?"

Laura nodded. "I never saw you in the pool."

"We had a pool at the house which I used before I moved out. I work out on the machines at the Y."

"You are in good shape."

Jo blushed, her eyes darting away from Laura's. "So are you."

"Oh well, wrestling with large animals helps." Laura laughed.

When they returned to the room, Jo changed into an oversized T-shirt in the bathroom. She felt overwhelmed with shyness mixed with intense desire. Was she right about Laura? Was the vet coming onto her or was she imagining what she wanted to happen?

In separate beds, propped up on pillows, they read. The words blurred on the page. Jo found herself rereading whole paragraphs and not absorbing the meaning. Once she looked up and found Laura looking back. Her eyes returned to the printed page as a flush climbed her neck and suffused her face. She knew she'd never be the one to cross the distance between the two beds. This was torture.

"She of faint heart never gets what she wants."

"What did you say?" Jo asked, hardly able to catch a breath.

"You heard right."

Now was the time to say she was involved with Gail. She should have made it clear from the beginning. She hadn't and now she knew she wouldn't. She wanted this as much as she was afraid of it.

The mattress moved when Laura slid in next to her. Jo marveled at the nerve it must have taken to cross that strip of carpet when the word lesbian had never been uttered.

Laura took the book out of her hands and looked at the cover. "Barbara Kingsolver. You can always count on her women not to compromise their ideals, even if it means they end up alone."

She sat very still, inhaling the clean odor of Laura's hair. The rest of her smelled of chlorine from the hot tub and pool.

"Are you all right with this?" Laura asked, meeting her eyes.

She nodded, watching with eyes open as Laura closed the distance between them. By the time their lips touched she'd shut out the view.

Slowly she slid down until she lay flat on the bed. Laura went with her as if they were attached. The kissing, at first gentle, grew increasingly urgent. Jo couldn't get enough of it.

When they separated enough to look at each other, both were breathing heavily. Leaning over, Jo kissed the soft winged space between the collar bone and neck.

"Whoever would have guessed?" Laura said with a smile.

Jo gave no answering smile. She was aware that she'd done this to Mark with Gail. She was certainly untrustworthy.

"Take your shirt off." Laura pulled up the hem. "I've been wanting to see you."

She'd never been a modest person. The features of her body were like the ones on her face. She had large breasts, fullsome hips and thighs, a rather large behind.

When Laura squirmed out of her nightie, Jo admired her lean, athletic looking body. Her breasts were only a handful, her legs long and lovely, her belly flat. How different yet alike they were.

Jo lay on her side, supporting her head with a hand, caressing the milky skin that glowed under her touch. Occasionally, she bent over and kissed Laura's shoulder or lips or neck or breasts. Slowly she worked her way toward the triangle of curls. Whenever Laura attempted to reciprocate, she whispered, "Not yet." Reaching the pubis, she burrowed into the depths.

Breathing heavily, Laura began to move under Jo's touch. She turned to face Jo and said in a hoarse voice, "You have to catch up. I'm way ahead of you."

Sighing with pleasure, Jo slipped an arm under Laura's neck and drew her close enough that their lips touched and their bodies came together. She felt Laura's hand move over her breasts, her hips, her backside. When the hand found its way between her legs, she knew she was ready.

Afterwards as they lay on their backs, Jo thought of the many different ways to make love. Neither had broken the silence that had followed orgasm, and Jo was loath to be the first.

"You are quite the lover," Laura said finally. She turned toward Jo. "Such wonderful breasts," she murmured.

Still unwilling to talk, Jo twined long fingers in Laura's hair and held her there. Gail had said much the same things when they first began making love. She knew she was good and attributed it to knowing her own body. "Years of masturbation," she said with a smile.

Laura burst into laughter.

The next morning Jo awoke to find Laura tucked into her arm. She lifted herself enough to see the digital clock by the bedside. "Time to get up."

Laura threw an arm over Jo and muttered, "I don't want to."

"Neither do I, but I promised I'd be at work tomorrow." She got up and made coffee. In the shower, she cleansed her hair and body. There must be no lingering scent of Laura.

The curtain moved and Laura got into the tub. "Let me wash your back," she said.

Jo smiled and handed her the soap. Then she washed Laura's hair and back and dried her off. They dressed, drank their coffee, and headed for the front door and airport shuttle.

Reality stared Jo in the face. It was virtually impossible to carry on an affair when neither lover knew the existence of another. Laura would want to call her at home and spend time with her, including whole days and evenings and nights. She would have to confess Gail to Laura to keep that from happening. There was no other way.

On the plane, they were able to sit next to one another. As they neared the county airport, Jo asked, "Is your brother meeting you?"

"No. Wendy is."

"Wendy who?" Jo asked.

Laura looked directly into her eyes. Jo knew with a certainty who Wendy was. She was Laura's Gail. "Oh." She laughed a little, hiding the jolt of pain. "And I thought I was the only guilty one."

"You too?" Laura lifted one fair eyebrow. "Connie's mother?"

She nodded. "Gail. Can we be friends, you and I?"

"I'd like that." Laura smiled a little. "Did you ever read *Other Women*?"

"One of my favorite books. Why?" The plane was descending. "I wish we could have had more than one night."

"Remember the woman at the health spa in Boston in the book?"

Jo searched her memory and came up with the scene. The protagonist, Caroline, and the woman at the spa had had anonymous sex without exchanging names, without getting involved in each other's lives. She nodded.

"I thought I could do that." The wheels hit the runway, bounced, and screamed in protest as the brakes took hold. "But we knew each other. It was already too late."

Laura's gray eyes were solemn. She squeezed Jo's hand. "Maybe we can do it again."

"I hope so," Jo said, returning the pressure.

Gail waited inside the airport, looking small and neat in

jeans and winter jacket. They exchanged grins and a hug before Gail started toward the luggage carousel.

Jo held her back. "Wait a minute. I have to introduce you to Laura. She's one of the vets at Boo's clinic. She was on the plane."

As the four of them waited for their baggage, Jo observed Wendy. Older than Laura, she was the same height, a strikingly handsome woman with dark hair streaked gray on the sides, and black flashing eyes. They looked such a good match that Jo at first surmised that her brief affair with Laura had been a casual fling. Listening to Wendy for only those few moments, though, told her there was an edge to this woman that she wouldn't want to cross.

XIV

"How's Connie?" Jo asked on the drive home.

"She was doing homework when I left. I think she missed you. I certainly did."

She didn't believe Connie had missed her, but let it go by without comment. "I can't begin to tell you how glad I am to be home. It was the weirdest week. Mom wasn't in the hospital. She conned Stan into telling us she'd had a stroke. I felt bad at first that she thought that was the only way to get Kim and me to come. But then she wanted the three of us to be close, and I let myself be lulled into admitting I left Mark because I was a lesbian. And, of course, she lost it. I guess our dad was gay. She kept him away from us, thinking it might be catching."

"You're kidding. I never told my folks. I don't know what I'll do with you when they visit." Gail sounded awed.

"Hasn't Connie told them?"

"She says she's too ashamed."

"I guess I won't get to meet them, huh?" She could always stay at Kim's.

"We'll worry about that when the time comes."

"The weather was a nice escape. What did you do while I was gone?"

"The usual. Worked, ate, slept. Can't wait to get you home."

They lugged Jo's suitcase into the house. Music drifted from Connie's closed bedroom door. Boo Boo lay on the bed she and Gail shared.

"Off, off," Gail said, putting the cat on the floor. "I don't want him in our room on our bed. There's hair everywhere." She shooed the feline out the door and closed it. The music faded.

"I told Connie a while back to turn down the volume or tune into classical. For the cat." Jo laughed.

Gail laughed too, then kissed her. "I've been wanting to do that since I saw you get off the plane."

Realizing she hadn't even thought of it herself, Jo felt a pang of guilt.

There were still a few hours left in the afternoon, and Jo read the Sunday paper before looking for a Joe Stanford in the phone book. She wanted to hang onto the hope that his name would be there. When it wasn't, she felt disappointed.

"It's like losing someone you'd just been given hope of finding. I didn't even know how much I looked forward to knowing my father."

Connie had walked into the room, unnoticed by Jo. "You never knew your father?"

Jo looked at the girl. "I must have once, but I was too young to remember him."

"What happened to him?" the girl asked with interest.

"He left. My mother wouldn't let him see me and Kim."

Connie's blue eyes grew darker in her pale face. "Why?"

"That wouldn't happen these days," Gail said.

"Wouldn't it?" she asked, glancing at Gail instead of Connie.

"Yeah," Connie said.

"He was gay. Our mother told us after all these years. I always thought he didn't want to see Kim or me."

Connie stared at her. "My dad didn't try to keep me away from my mom, even after he found out."

"Lucky you."

Connie snorted a laugh. "Yeah, lucky me. I've got a queer mom and a dad with his own family." When her mother put a hand on her arm, she shrugged it off and went into the kitchen.

Jo met Gail's eyes. "She missed me, huh?"

Gail shrugged and followed Connie into the kitchen. Jo took the portable phone upstairs to the bedroom and called information, asking for a Joseph Stanford in communities around the state. She came downstairs with listings in Milwaukee and Madison.

Connie was stretched out on the couch reading a book, which made Jo remember the James Herriot book, *All Creatures Great and Small,* that she had bought for the girl.

She produced it from her book bag. "Here. This is a good read. I think you'll like it." She handed the book to Connie, who took it and immediately read the flap.

"Thanks," Connie said.

"Is your mom in the kitchen?" she asked.

"Hey, I'm sorry about your dad. You know, your not knowing him," the girl said.

Jo perched at the other end of the couch. "That's okay. I guess you don't miss what you don't have. I do have a stepdad."

"Yeah. Do you like him?" The girl looked interested.

"He's okay. His name is Stan. Actually, he seemed more like a fixture than anything else."

"He didn't take you places or talk to you?" Connie asked.

She'd thought Connie was plain when she first met her. Now she noticed how well proportioned her features were, a perfectly appointed but miniature adult. "I suppose he did."

"Did you like your mom when you were a kid?"

Jo shrugged. "My mom wasn't much interested in me. Maybe I reminded her of my father. I guess I look like him."

"She didn't love you?" Connie asked, appalled.

"Maybe my perception was wrong. Maybe she didn't know how to show her love."

"Didn't anyone love you?"

"My sister, Kim. We loved each other. I'm sure our mother loved us in her own way."

"I wish I had a real sister."

"Well, you have two parents who love you." She went into the kitchen.

Plunging into the work week, Jo felt as if she'd never left as she paged through the many messages on her desk.

Walter brought her coffee and filled her in on the events of the past week. He looked at her over his glasses. "How is your mother?"

Not wanting to explain, she said, "Better."

"Good. I'm glad you're back. I had Carol calling applicants to fill job positions."

She smiled. "Maybe we should give her an office and hire another receptionist."

"If we get any busier, we will."

Carol poked her head in the door and said hello. "How's your mother?"

"Pretty good, considering," she said.

"Come on in and join us."

"I can't. Clients." She jerked her head toward the waiting room. "Good to see you where you belong, Jo."

Walter unfolded his pudgy frame and stood up. "We missed you."

At the end of the day she returned to her office after a trip to the women's room. Outside, the wind had picked up, sending sleet slanting across the parking lot. Yesterday morning she had left Florida in warm sunshine. As she readied to leave, she listened to her voice mail.

"Hi, Laura Bender here. Give me a call when you get a chance. I'll be at the clinic late this evening."

Setting down her purse, she phoned the clinic and asked for Laura.

Laura picked up. "Hi. How's it going?"

"Busy day. How about you?"

"The same. I wondered if you'd like to meet for lunch tomorrow."

She checked the date in her appointment book. "Where?"

"How about the Thai place?"

Jo hurried to her car, sleet stinging her face. Starting the engine, she turned on the heat. Even though the fan would blow only cold air until the motor warmed, it gave an illusion of heat.

She sat thinking while sleet hissed against the car. There was nowhere to go with this affair. She wished she'd met Laura earlier when she'd have had the chance to choose. She briefly wondered what Gail would do. Throw her out, that's what.

"I'm a fool," she said aloud, putting the Sebring in gear. The wheels burned through the ice and the car lurched forward.

The kitchen glowed under a warm, yellow light. Gail was heating up leftovers, while Connie set the table. Boo sat in the middle of the floor. It was the perfect homey setting. Jo shut the door behind her and took it in with a smile.

"How was your day?" Gail asked, pursing her lips in a long distance kiss.

"Busy. And yours?" She shrugged out of her wet coat and hung it on the hall tree in the small mud room.

"Not bad, considering it's a Monday." Gail remarked cheerfully.

"Anybody want to know about my day?" Connie asked, scooping up the cat.

"Let me change first," Jo said.

Sitting down at the table a few minutes later, she looked hungrily at the food.

"Okay, tell us," Gail said to her daughter.

"It's too boring," Connie remarked, reaching for the bowl of steaming potatoes.

Out of the corner of her eye, Jo saw the cat launch itself through the air. He landed near the meatloaf, startling them all.

"Shut that animal in his kennel," Gail snapped. "He's got to learn to stay off the table and counters."

Connie grabbed the feline and shoved him in the kennel. Gail swung the kitchen door closed to shut out his complaints.

"He's just a cat, Ma. He doesn't get it."

"Well, he better get it or he'll spend every meal in that cage."

"So what was so boring about your day?" Jo asked.

"Mimi spends all her time with Bucky. He's such a dope," the girl said vehemently.

"Who are Mimi and Bucky?" Jo said.

"Mimi was my best friend, and Bucky is this big jerk who farts in class and thinks it's funny."

Gail and Jo stared at Connie. "He does what in class?"

"Farts. Then he blames the mousy girl who sits next to him. All she does is blush."

"Is Mimi in this class?" Gail asked.

"No, but I told her and she just laughed. He's on the freshman basketball team. That makes him a bigshot."

Jo sped back to her junior high school days. Even level-headed girls turned silly in the presence of the most dismally immature boys. She wondered then what her friends saw in their inanities. "Is there anyone you like?"

"Yeah. I like James. He makes me laugh."

"Is he cute?" Gail asked.

"No, and he doesn't do sports. He's funny and smart."

"You haven't had Mimi over in ages," Gail said.

"I'm supposed to bring her here? She'll ask questions." Connie looked incredulous.

Gail chewed on her lip.

Their plates were empty. Jo said, "I'll clean up."

Connie stalked off to her room. Gail put the food away as Jo loaded the dishwasher. "She never brings anyone home anymore. Mimi used to practically live here. She's ashamed of me."

"And me," Jo added. "Maybe I should get an apartment."

"You're not serious."

"Yes, I am. I can come and stay on the weekends when Connie's at her dad's." She felt a twinge of unexpected anticipation.

"This is what you want, isn't it?"

"This is what we should have done," she replied. "We can live together when she goes off to college."

Gail wiped the counters down with more vigor than necessary. "Five years is a long time."

Jo turned up the heat and slid further under the electric blanket. She had switched off the reading light and lay listening to the wind and the sleet clattering at the windows. It was still November. She hoped December would bring snow.

Gail had agreed to her moving out after a quiet, fierce argument, and now loneliness gripped her.

"You're wrong about Connie," Gail said.

"Think about it. Her father has a new wife, new kids, and then I move in and you have a new partner. She's shoved to the side."

"You didn't take her place. You couldn't."

"This is her house and yours. I'll visit when she's at her dad's. She'll bring her friends over again."

Jo wasn't sure how much of what she had said was heartfelt and how much was made up to excuse her leaving.

XV

The Thai restaurant was dark and smelled of cooking oil. Laura raised a hand from a rear booth. Jo slid into the bench seat opposite the vet.

"Hi. Sorry I'm a little late. I had a job applicant I couldn't get rid of."

"I haven't been waiting long. I always have the buffet. What about you?"

"Sounds good. Are you ready?"

Back at the booth, she eyed Laura over a bowl of watery soup. "Do you live with Wendy?"

"I live with my dog," Laura replied.

"What's his name?"

"Buddy. Somebody abandoned him at the clinic when he

was a pup. I take him to work with me." Laura gave her a hint of smile. "How's Boo Boo?"

"He landed right in the middle of the dining room table last night. Gail was traumatized."

Laura laughed. "Cats can learn. Don't give up on him."

Their soup bowls emptied, they were about to return to the buffet when Jo saw someone waving in their direction from across the room. She recognized Brad. "That's my brother-in-law. I think he wants to tell me something."

"Better go find out," Laura said.

Brad got to his feet and introduced her to the other man and woman at the table. "Phil and Audrey Compton."

She shook their hands. "I've been meaning to call you, Ms. Compton. I need a lawyer, and Brad recommended you."

"Call me Audrey." The woman fished out a business card and handed it to Jo.

"Thanks." She turned to Brad. "What time are you picking up Kim tonight?"

"Seven-ten," Brad replied. "The kids are excited."

"I'll call her sometime tomorrow."

Jo filled a plate and carried it back to the booth. "Brad's an attorney as is my soon-to-be ex. He recommended that woman for a divorce lawyer. Audrey Compton. Do you know her?"

"Nope," Laura said. "I ordered us decaf."

"Thanks." She wanted to say something about the night at the Hilton but failed to think of anything appropriate. "I'm moving again. Gail and I decided it was better for Connie if we didn't live together."

Laura put her coffee cup down. "I know of a condo for rent, six months, fully furnished. One of our clients spends her winters in the Bahamas."

"Where is it?" she asked.

"On the river. Nice location. I can give you the name of the agency that's representing her. They'll show it to you."

"How much?"

"Five hundred. Cheap, considering. She wants someone to look after the place."

"I'm interested," she said.

Kim called her at the office in the morning. "Let's go to lunch. I'll buy you a bagel at the library."

"Aren't you the generous one? Okay. See you at noon."

Jo was drinking coffee at one of the tables when Kim arrived with Sydney in tow. Syd clung to her mother.

"She thinks I might disappear again," Kim said as Jo hugged them both.

Sydney smeared creamed cheese on her cheeks, eating the bagel her mother cut up for her. Jo watched the child with amusement.

"How was the rest of your visit?" Jo asked.

"I couldn't wait to leave. Mother wants to be close, but she doesn't know how. Neither do I."

"She slammed the door on that long ago." Jo spread more creamed cheese on her bagel and bit into it.

Squirming in her chair, Sydney looked around restlessly. "Finish that piece, baby, and you can go see the children's books," Kim told her. But the little girl leaned into her mother and shook her head. "She's been like a leech since I got home."

"I'm moving again, Kim."

"What? You're not serious."

"I am serious. We decided it would be better for Connie if I didn't live there."

"I just moved you in," Kim complained.

"There are only clothes. The new place is furnished. I can do it myself over Thanksgiving, while Gail and Connie are visiting Gail's parents."

"You're not going with them?"

"I won't even answer that. I've got an appointment with

a realtor to look at this condo after work tonight." She smiled at her sister. "Think about it. Freedom."

"I didn't know you felt so caged in."

"Neither did I." She watched as her sister hoisted Sydney onto her lap. "Where did you learn to be such a good mother?"

"It was easy. I did whatever Mother didn't." Kim cuddled the child, who sucked her thumb and leaned against her mother. "What happened at the Hilton?"

"None of your beeswax, and this time I mean it." Jo smiled.

"Aha. I thought so."

Before leaving, she gave Kim the list of Joe Stanford phone numbers that she'd gotten through information and the library's assortment of phone books.

She parked next to the realtor's car outside the condominium complex. Shaking the woman's hand, she followed her out of the cold wind blowing off the river into the one story unit. Before she closed the door, she knew she wanted to live there. The beiges soothed her, the bright pictures on the wall caught her interest, the comfortable furniture relaxed her. There were only a few rooms. A lushly carpeted living room with a gas fireplace and a river view, a large, efficient kitchen with a highly polished wood floor, two bedrooms where the carpet hushed footsteps. Each had their own bath. The larger bedroom's bath held a shower/tub/whirlpool enclosure. Outside the living room a screened-in porch faced the river. Between condo and garage was a small walled-in brick patio and flower patch. There was also a basement complete with a carpeted area that held a TV, furniture, and a built-in bar, a separate, tiled laundry room, and a bathroom with a shower.

She turned a complete circle in the living room and sat down on the pale beige leather couch. "I'll take it."

The realtor's frosty smile told her nothing. "No pets, no roommates, no other furnishings."

"None."

"Here's the six month lease. Read it over. You must be moved out by June first. Our professional cleaning service will clean once a week. You will pay them. Send the monthly rent check to our offices."

Jo scanned the print, signed the paper, wrote a check for two months rent, and handed them to the realtor. "I plan to move in Thanksgiving weekend."

"This is a wonderful deal. Mrs. Bannister wants someone here to keep an eye on the place." The woman gave her another cool smile, which she returned in kind. The implication was not lost.

"I'd do that anyway." She was ready to leave.

At home, Gail waited dinner for her, the warm kitchen redolent. She stood inside the door, thinking how much she would miss coming home to a good meal and conversation.

Gail glanced her way as she fished a casserole out of the oven. "How was the place?"

"Nice," she replied, curbing her enthusiasm. "I signed on for six months." Bending down she patted the cat meowing at her feet. "Have you told Connie?"

"Yeah, I did. She's in her room, doing homework. You want to call her down for dinner?"

"Sure." She took the stairs two at a time, changed her clothes, and knocked on Connie's door. "Time to eat," she yelled over the music. No answer. She knocked again.

"I'm coming," Connie shouted.

Gail sat at the table, her face averted, but Jo saw the quivering lips when she sat down. "Aw, honey. I'll be here most of the time or you there."

Gail sniffed, straightened, and drew in a shaky breath. "I know."

She felt like a turncoat, excited because she was going to be on her own. What if she moved into the condo only to be terribly lonely? And if Gail found someone else, what then?

Connie plunked herself down on her chair and eyed the food. "What is that stuff?"

"Dinner, you mean?" Gail said, her tone a warning.

"Yeah." The girl's raised her eyes briefly and looked at Jo.

"Try it, you might like it," Jo said.

"I think I'll just have a peanut butter sandwich."

"Oh, no. You'll eat some of the casserole first." Gail dumped a large spoonful on the girl's plate.

Bending over, Connie took a dainty bite.

Jo held up her plate. "Please," she said, and Gail spooned on the potpie, a mix of beans and corn and ground meat under the breaded top. Taking a taste, she said enthusiastically, "Good, excellent."

"Mom says you're moving out." Connie's voice came out flat, expressionless.

Raising her eyes to meet the girl's gaze, she caught a blaze of blue before Connie looked away. "For a few months."

"Why?" The rage surprised Jo.

"I thought, we thought," she glanced at Gail for help but got none, "you might be more comfortable in your own home. I know we embarrass you. You can bring your friends here again."

"I knew it. Mom's going to blame me." Connie hunched further over her plate.

"No, I'm not. It's Jo's choice to move out, her decision, not yours or mine." Gail gave Jo an angry glare.

"It's too late," she said, momentarily regretting her choice. "I signed the lease and paid for a couple of months."

They ate while the cat circled. "If that animal jumps up on the table again, he's out of here," Gail warned.

Pushing her chair back, Connie grabbed Boo Boo and shut

him in the kitchen. "You hate him, don't you, Mom?" She plopped down on her chair again while the cat raised his voice in complaint.

"No. I just don't want him eating with us," Gail snapped.

This was her fault, Jo thought. She said, "I thought you'd be pleased."

"I am. You never cared about us anyway." Connie glared at her across the table.

Jo thought back to her youth, trying to link this behavior with some memory. She dredged up a picture of her mother after she married Stan, before she drove off on the honeymoon, giving her a wine soaked hug, telling her to be good, that she'd be back in a month. "Why can't we go with you?" she'd asked. Everyone had laughed.

"That's not fair and certainly not true," she said.

"It is true," the girl sneered. "I just get in your way." Connie stood up abruptly and took her half full plate to the kitchen.

Jo stared at her back helplessly as she disappeared through the swinging door. "I can't win."

"I told you she liked you," Gail said accusingly.

"She has a damn strange way of showing it."

When Kim called, Jo was watching a program on public television with Gail. Comfortably ensconced on the sofa, an afghan thrown over their legs, they lay in the opposite directions. She picked up the phone and pressed it to her ear.

"Hi. I've got news, Jo."

"What?" Then it dawned on her and she inquired with lofted brows, "Our father?"

"Yeah. I made some inquiries, talked to his roommate. He moved to Milwaukee nearly ten years ago."

Ten years ago she was in her early thirties. "And?"

"He owns a new and used bookstore."

"No kidding." She grabbed a pen and paper. "What's the name of it?"

"The Written Word. I thought we should talk to him together."

"I never thought I'd get a chance to know the man, did you?"

"No. It's sort of scary. We don't know anything about him."

"What if we don't like him?"

"What if he doesn't like us?" Kim said.

"Let's call over Thanksgiving weekend. That'll give us time to get used to the idea. Thanks, Kim."

"You were the one who found the numbers."

Gail was looking at her, waiting. "Well?"

"Kim found our father."

"Are you excited?"

"It's another complication. He was here until ten years ago. He could have made contact."

Thanksgiving was a week away. As Jo ate toast and drank coffee the next morning, Connie and Gail plodded around the kitchen half-awake.

"When's your dad picking you up?" Gail asked her daughter.

"After school." Connie threw them both a baleful look. "You two can have a weekend of unabated bliss."

Jo burst into laughter. "Are you practicing your vocabulary?" She realized she'd miss the kid. Connie never failed to raise some kind of emotion in her.

The girl flipped her chin in Jo's direction, "And then she'll be gone. She won't have to put up with me anymore."

"My name is Jo." Had Connie ever called her that? "And I'll miss your wildly erroneous statements."

"What does that mean?" The kid stared at her.

"Look it up."

XVI

She called Audrey Compton's office and made an appointment to see her over the lunch hour. "I think it'll be pretty cut and dried, but Brad thought I should have a lawyer. Do you know Mark Morrison?"

"I've met him."

"He's a decent kind of guy."

"Well, divorce is all about dividing up the money. It's a leveling act. Sometimes I think we don't know ourselves or anyone else until we own something together and one or the other wants out."

She hung up the phone and sat down in front of the computer to read her e-mails. There was one from Walter: Coffee in my office at nine.

Carrying her cup, she crossed the few feet of carpeting to Walter's corner office, nodding at the few people in the waiting room. Rapping on Walter's door, she pushed it open.

"Come in, come in," he said, getting up.

Carol sat in one of the chairs. Jo took the other. "Something wrong with the phone?"

"I don't know. I haven't been on it." Walter grinned. "I've been thinking about your suggestion that we give Carol some of our work load." He leaned over the desk and filled their coffee cups.

"I can do some of the calling for you out at the front desk," Carol said.

Jo looked at the younger woman. She thought of herself a few years ago when Walter invited her to share the job responsibilities. The business was growing. "I've got a bunch of clients to phone. I'd be glad to pass that along."

"You pick 'em, I'll call 'em," Carol said. She got up. "I better go back to my desk before someone makes off with my computer."

Walter said, "Stay a minute, Jo." When they were alone, he remarked, "If she does well, maybe we should give her an office and hire someone else. Do you think there's enough work?"

"Let's give this a try. We'll know soon enough."

"Come on," Gail said over breakfast on Saturday. "I want to see the place. Is it awful or something?"

She hesitated. "Okay. Let's go."

Jo pushed the garage door opener and the dark green double door slid up on its track. Parking her car inside, she unlocked the door to the kitchen, then threw the keys on the inlaid countertop.

Gail walked through the rooms without saying a thing. Jo waited, staring out the living room windows at the river. "What do you think?" she asked when Gail joined her.

"I don't know what to say. It's out of my league."

Putting an arm around Gail, she lied, "I wish I hadn't signed that lease."

"Will you be able to relax here? It's so posh."

"I hope you'll spend some weekends with me."

"We'll be in different households again, just like old times," Gail said with a sigh.

"Except that I won't have to answer to anyone," she pointed out. "I can see you whenever I want."

Gail moved away. "Makes me sound like a convenience."

"No more than I am. Shall we spend the night here?"

"I don't think so. Connie won't know how to get hold of me, and Boo will be lonesome."

"Why don't we at least consecrate the bed?" She began walking Gail backward to the bedroom.

But the room didn't feel like hers. After pulling down the comforter, she looked at the expensive satiny sheets and paused.

Gail followed her glance. "We can't. Let's go home and do it on our own sheets."

"No," she said firmly, lowering Gail to the cool silky fabric. Was she supposed to use her own linens? She hadn't asked. She had no sheets the size of the bed anyway.

Gail pulled her down on top of her. "God, what luxury," she said with another sigh.

Kissing her mouth and breasts, Jo buried her face between their fullness and breathed deeply, contentedly. Her hand slid down Gail's ribcage, over her hips and up the inside of her thighs. Gail's sharp intake of breath, her readiness to the touch, triggered Jo's passion. She lifted her head, squirmed her way upward, and pressed Gail to her. They melded as one.

Afterwards, they sat in the huge whirlpool tub, side by side, touching. Gail leaned her head back and closed her eyes, a thin line of perspiration beading her upper lip.

Jo leaned over and ran a tongue over the droplets. She placed a hand between Gail's legs. "Want to?"

"Again? No, I'm quite satisfied." Gail opened an eye and smiled at her. "You can try, though."

The tub's surface was unyielding and slippery. Jo gave up after a few attempts to find a comfortable position. "Later," she said. "You still want to go home?"

"Don't you think the cat will miss us? Besides, we don't have anything to eat or drink."

"There's wine in the car. I'll go get it," Jo offered.

"We can always order out."

Gail slid deeper into the hot water.

Grabbing a robe she found in the closet and sliding wet bare feet into her tennies, Jo got the wine. In the kitchen she went through drawers until she found a corkscrew, then searched cupboards for wine glasses. Carrying the glasses and open wine bottle, she returned to the hot tub, filled the glasses, and settled into the depths.

Afterwards, they ordered pizza and ate it in the kitchen. Turning on the gas fireplace, they settled into the leather sofa and watched a movie on one of the many cable channels. When they finally returned to the bed, an owl was hooting outside. Lying in the dark, Jo talked about her meeting with Audrey Compton earlier in the week.

Sitting in Audrey's plush office at noon, she'd felt uncomfortable. Mark had yet to serve her papers. "Am I supposed to start proceedings? I thought he would do that. I was the one who left."

"If you can agree on a settlement, you'll save a lot of money in attorney fees."

In the end, she'd paid the retainer and told Audrey she'd contact her when she heard from Mark.

Gail's voice sounded sleepy. "Why are you so reluctant to file?"

"I left. I thought I'd give him the courtesy of filing first."

Gail said, "I guess you'll have to do what you're comfortable with, but it sounds like convoluted thinking to me."

"Who filed first, you or Conrad?"

"He did. No compunctions on his part." And she fell asleep.

Jo lay awake awhile, listening for the owl and hearing only the wind.

Gail and Connie left to visit Gail's parents in Chicago on Wednesday. Jo worked late, bringing her files up to date, knowing they were already gone. She had promised to look after Boo Boo.

Coming home to the mewling cat and an empty house left her sad. She would spend Thanksgiving with Kim's family the next day. Having been assigned the dessert, she had picked up the ingredients for pumpkin and mince meat pies. Now she put them together while the cat twined around her legs, tripping her up. Twice he jumped up on the counter to get her attention. Both times she shoved him off with a sweep of her arm. He fell to the floor with a thump and an indignant meow. "Off. Stay off."

Then she felt mean and bent to pat him, and he bit her. She smacked him and he swatted at her. She laughed. When he persisted, though, she took a newspaper and batted it at him. He backed off. "You are a little tiger," she said as his tail swished back and forth.

She packed her personal belongings and curled up on the couch with a peanut butter sandwich and a book.

The next morning she put the pies on the floor on the

passenger side. Loading the suitcases and boxes in the trunk and backseat, she drove to Kim and Brad's. The day was windy, spewing snow against her windshield. Pulling into the driveway, she carried the pies to the door.

Max let her in and took the pies from her while Lauren twirled in front of her, showing off her new shirt and pants. The twins hung from Jo's arms and legs, babbling, as she scooped up a sticky Sydney.

She hadn't seen Kim since their lunch in the library. With her entourage in tow, she entered the kitchen. Her heart nearly stopped, then plugged on faithfully. Mark sat at the large table with Brad and Kim. He looked thin and tense. Their heads swung toward her. Only the kids kept talking.

Mark stood up, his blue eyes so intense she felt herself shrinking. "Hi. I just dropped in. I'm leaving now," he said.

"We've been begging him to stay for dinner," Brad said, looking at Jo.

"Why don't you?" she murmured to Mark. "Are you going to Ted's?"

"Ted's out of town."

"Don't leave for my sake." Engulfed with sadness, she wondered if this was a set-up. She put Sydney down.

"Want a drink?" Kim asked, reading her confusion.

"Love one." She got down the vodka and tonic and made her own.

The twins pulled on her for attention, waving a deck of cards.

"In a minute," she promised.

The long pine table with benches served as the kitchen table. With the twins on either side of her and Lauren across and next to Mark, she shuffled the deck. "Rummy?"

"Yeah," the twins said in unison.

"No peeking," Mark said to Lauren teasingly.

"Aren't you playing, Dad?" Lauren asked.

"Nope, I'll help your mom."

"I can help. You take my place, Brad," Jo said.

"No, you're a guest," Brad said firmly.

She dealt out the cards, placed the remainder of the deck down with the top card face up next to it. "You start, Ben."

The twins had no concept of time. In between hands, they disappeared under the table and had to be hauled out. Even Lauren needed a reminder when it was her turn. The girl giggled whenever Mark pretended to peer under a card before he drew. Jo, who liked a game to move along, resigned herself to the slow pace and laughed with them. She kept an eye on the twins' hands, making sure they missed no plays. After Anna accumulated a hundred points, the designated winning score, Jo called it quits.

When Max announced a Charlie Brown special, the kids deserted en masse, and she found herself sitting across from Mark.

"How've you been?" he asked.

She started to say fine. The words caught in her throat. "Okay. And you?"

"Busy. I miss you." He added, "Maybe I miss having someone to talk to."

"You didn't just stop in, did you?" she asked.

"No," he admitted, "Brad said you'd be here alone."

Nodding, she thought of all that had happened since she'd last talked to him. Once she'd shared her life with him, her days, her thoughts. Now she couldn't think of an appropriate thing to say. "I better see if Kim needs help."

Kim didn't, though. In her usual self sufficient way she had dinner under control. Jo found her observing the dining room table with a hostess' eye. The house was warm, the aromas almost edible. The kids and Brad had gathered in the den in front of the TV.

Jo wandered into the empty living room where a fire roared in the hearth. She sat in a reclining chair with the newspaper on her lap and stared at the flames. Barney lay on the rug in front of the fire, panting. She wasn't sure where Mark was.

After dinner, Brad suggested bridge. They fell into an old pattern. For years they had made a foursome, Jo and Mark paired against Kim and Brad.

It felt like old times — comfortable and pleasant. She noted that her new life was only comfy and easy when she and Gail were alone. When she'd gone with Gail to Kim's for dinner, there had been an almost palpable awkwardness. But then she and Mark had shared many dinners with Kim and Brad. They'd been friends from the beginning. She altered the balance by changing partners.

It was midnight before she went back to Gail's and fell into bed, shutting the door in the cat's face. Boo had been alone all day and wouldn't be ignored. He meowed so loudly, she got up and let him in. Curling up on Gail's pillow, he purred contentedly. Jo smiled, thinking how annoyed Gail would be. She'd have to change the pillowcase before Sunday.

XVII

The Friday after Thanksgiving, Kim phoned the bookstore from her house as Jo looked on. The kids were outside, playing in the few inches of snow that had fallen.

"Joe Stanford?" her sister said, smiling encouragingly at Jo. "My name is Kim. My sister, Jo, and I are looking for our father." There was a long pause, and Kim winked reassuringly at Jo. "I'm fine. Married with five kids. Yeah, you've got five grandchildren who'd love to meet you. Jo and I would too." Kim listened with a half smile.

Jo rocked from foot to foot. Why did she care what he thought of her?

"When? Next weekend. We'll talk it over and get back to you. You could come here. You're more than welcome."

Another pause while Jo waited, now with a frown of concentration on her face. "We'll let you know in the next day or two. Want to talk to Jo?"

She started to protest, but Kim thrust the phone at her. Putting the receiver to her ear, she managed a hello.

"Hi, Jo." A deep voice said. "How'd you find me?"

"Through information. Why? Were you hiding?"

"I've been undercover from your mother for thirty-eight years. I promised her I'd stay out of your lives. What do you know about me?"

"Mom told us you were gay, after she found out I was."

He sighed. "Sorry. I suppose she blamed that on me too."

"She doesn't believe it's hereditary." She felt sudden anger. "Why did you never get in touch with us?"

"Your mother's wrath is a terrible thing." His voice was deep, warm.

She barked a laugh. "Isn't it? We grew up sidestepping it."

"I couldn't have helped you, honey. I did a tapdance to avoid it myself."

A slow smile curled across her face as she turned to Kim, who raised her eyebrows and said softly, "Better late than never."

They would go.

That afternoon, Kim helped her carry her personal belongings to the condo and put them away. Kim was as impressed as she and Gail had been.

"It's so elegantly furnished. I wish I had this woman's taste. It is a woman, isn't it?"

Jo nodded. "Mrs. Bannister. She spends the winter in the Bahamas, lucky woman." She fell back in a deep leather chair.

"How did you find this place?" Kim tried out the other leather chair.

"Mrs. Bannister left a note on the bulletin board at the animal clinic. Laura Bender told me about it."

"Laura. Is that who you were with at the Thai place?"

"Brad told on me."

"It doesn't count when he tells me. It's not like he called Gail or Mark. By the way, did you have a good time yesterday?" she asked casually.

"Yeah but next time let me know if he's been invited, will you?"

"It was sort of a spur of the moment thing. We knew he was going to be alone. You still care about Mark. I knew you wouldn't mind."

"It makes me uncomfortable, pretending nothing has changed."

Kim looked at her. "He's waiting for you to come back, you know."

"Well, don't encourage him. I'm not going back. It wouldn't be fair to him or me," she snapped, her eyes on the river. An eagle soared into view and dropped like a stone. "Look, look!"

"What, what?" Kim jumped to her feet, alongside Jo.

"An eagle catching a fish. See it." God, she was going to like it here.

That night, though, Jo couldn't bring herself to leave the cat. She stopped in to double check his food and water, and he meowed so plaintively that she stayed. She watched a video with the feline curled up next to her on the couch, and when she climbed into bed, he hopped onto the comforter next to her. She awoke the next morning with him curled around her head, kneading her skull with the very paws she'd paid to have declawed.

Saturday morning she sat on the edge of the bed, looking out at the snow covered yards and feeling out of sorts. Promising herself she'd finalize her move to the condo, she felt a disconcerting loneliness, knowing she wouldn't be here when Gail and Connie returned on Sunday. Maybe she should have dinner ready for them when they returned, though. She'd leave it in the fridge with a note.

It gave her energy to have something to do. She had to grocery shop anyway in order to stock the condo with something to eat next week. She decided to make a double batch of creamy rigatoni and take some with her.

When the phone rang, she jumped with surprise. The silence of the empty house had settled into her, the only conversations going on between herself and Boo Boo. She picked up the phone.

"So there you are," Gail said in a breathy whisper. "I called the condo."

"The cat was lonesome," she explained. "How's it going?"

"Fine."

"Why are you whispering then?"

"I don't want to wake anyone up. It's early. Besides, I wanted to tell you how much I miss you, and I can't do that when there are people listening."

"I miss you, too. When are you coming home? I thought I'd leave you some supper."

"Can't you be there too?"

"Sure, but that's not what my moving out was all about."

"I know. You can spend the week nights at the condo. I want you to stay Sunday night."

"Okay. I talked to my father yesterday."

"Did you?" Gail said. "What was that like?"

"Kim and I are going to see him next weekend. Want to come along?"

"I'll see. I hear somebody in the kitchen. I've got to go. I love you."

"Me too."

She talked to the cat while she fixed coffee and toast. "So furball, even if you had to give up part of your toes, I bet you don't miss living under the porch." But when she left, he tried to follow her through the door. She tossed a cat treat across the room and hurried out.

The sun glinted off the inch or two of snow. She put on sunglasses. A cold, more normal winter had been forecast, in contrast to the warmer ones of the past few years. She had always liked the snow. Both she and Gail cross country skied, but Gail laughed at her because she enjoyed shoveling and blowing the snow. As she backed out of the driveway she'd cleared late yesterday, she almost wished she'd never met Laura. Then maybe she wouldn't have moved out.

From the condo she phoned the clinic. Laura answered. "I was just getting ready to leave, me and Buddy here. What are you doing?"

"Moving into the condo. It's wonderful. The real estate lady said no pets, but Mrs. Bannister must have a pet or she wouldn't have put a notice on your bulletin board."

"She does. A Westie. Cutest little dog you ever saw. Also the most spoiled animal in the world. Jumps on everything and everyone. No manners, but he gets away with it because he's such a charmer."

"I guess I wouldn't want to rent to someone with pets either, but why put a notice in an animal clinic then?"

"Well, it worked, didn't it? I'd like to see you," Laura said bluntly, sending goosebumps racing across Jo's skin.

"Why don't you come over for dinner Monday?" Her heart thumped a little harder, afraid Gail would find out.

"All right. What time?"

"Six? Six-thirty?" She didn't ask what Laura's plans were over the weekend or where she had gone for Thanksgiving. She assumed she spent her holidays and free time with Wendy. She didn't want to dwell on their infidelity too much.

When she hung up, she put her things away, turned on the gas fireplace, and settled in one of the leather chairs with a book. She'd gone through Mrs. Bannister's CD collection and filled the slots with the fine selection of baroque composers:

Vivaldi, Bach, Albinoni, Telemann, Corelli, Scarlatti. She felt herself relaxing, melting into the soft leather, becoming a part of it. Outside, the wind sent a thin layer of snow skimming over the ground, and waves whipped across the river under a steel gray sky.

But when the light dimmed outside, she headed for Gail's and the cat, wondering how long she'd feel torn between the house and condo. On the way, she picked up a video to watch that night.

Kim had sent home leftovers from Thanksgiving dinner. She heated them in the microwave and took her plate to the sofa in front of the TV. Having looked forward to this time alone, she never expected it to drag like this.

When Gail and Connie pulled into the driveway the next afternoon, Jo had put the finishing touches on the creamy rigatoni, made a salad, and baked a batch of brownies.

Connie banged through the door first. "I thought you moved out."

"Good to see you too," Jo said, holding the door open for Gail.

"Jeez, I didn't mean anything," the girl said as she brushed against Jo on her way inside. She dropped her suitcase and picked up Boo. "Poor kitty. You won't be alone anymore."

"He wasn't alone. I was here every night." Then Gail staggered inside, weighed down by her suitcase. Jo took it from her. "Did you take your whole wardrobe?"

Gail laughed. "Just about. You never know what the weather's going to be in Chicago."

"Cold this time of year," Jo said, picking up both bags and depositing them in the dining room.

"Smells good in here." Gail picked up the lid on the creamy sauce and peeked inside. "I'm starved."

"Me too," Connie said, rubbing her face in the cat's fur. "Did you miss me, Boo?" The feline purred loudly in answer.

Jo laughed. "He's vibrating."

Connie carried her suitcase and the cat upstairs, talking nonsense.

Gail gave Jo a kiss then. "Thanks for being here. I was dreading coming home to a house without you."

"Did you have a good time?" Jo asked.

"Yeah, we did. We shopped, went to the art museum, saw the relatives. It was fun. And you?" Gail paused before picking up her suitcase.

"Kind of lonesome."

"It'll be more lonesome once you're gone." Gail's eyes searched her face.

"I know." But Jo was thinking about Monday night when Laura was coming for dinner. Her pulse sped at the thought of what might happen.

At dinner she brought up the planned meeting with her father.

"You're really going to see him?" Connie asked. "After all these years."

"Yep. He was there until after Kim was born. I think I was three or four when he left. I just don't remember him. Do you recall anything from when you were three or four?"

"Maybe you don't want to remember. Maybe they had terrible fights," Connie persisted, "he and your mother."

"Connie," Gail said.

"They probably did. He said the wrath of my mother was a fearsome thing." She laughed again. "And it is."

"He could have fought to see you," Connie said. "Mine would have."

"Yours didn't have to," Gail pointed out.

"Maybe he didn't want to." Jo wondered what kind of chance a gay man had of getting visitation rights back then. Now gay couples were having kids of their own. He might have thought it was better if he didn't even try. Or maybe her mother had made it so unpleasant he'd completely backed off. She probably would never really know.

"You must be excited," Gail said, "after all these years."

"I am. It doesn't seem real."

XVIII

Monday flew by, and Jo left work promptly at five. She wanted to put dinner together before Laura arrived. Caught in traffic, she inched along until she reached the condo complex and whipped into the driveway.

Unlocking the kitchen door, she stepped inside. The place felt like it belonged to someone else. She hurried into the bedroom and changed from her suit into cotton slacks and shirt. Barefoot, she turned on public radio and padded into the kitchen.

At six o'clock the dining table was set with candles, the sauce warming on the stove, the salad made.

While waiting for Laura, she paged through the newspaper, trying without succeeding to concentrate.

When the phone rang, she jumped to answer it. "Hi," Gail said.

"Hi. What's up?"

"I wish you were here."

"Me too," she said, listening for a knock on the door. "What are you doing? Where's Connie?" She heard the cat meow.

"She's in her room with her friend, Mimi."

"That's good." The day she left Connie asked a friend over.

"It's not you," Gail said, reading her tone. "It's us she finds embarrassing. All teenagers find the sexuality of their parents a shameful thing."

She started to say it was the nature of their sexuality that embarrassed Connie when the doorbell rang, a mellow ding dong that Gail had to hear. "Got to go."

"Who's there?" Gail asked.

"I don't know."

"Call me later."

"I'm going out after I eat."

"Want company?"

"I have to get used to not seeing you during the week. I'll call when I get back." She hung up and hurried to the door.

Laura stood on the stoop, cheeks and nose red from the cold. "I thought maybe you forgot I was coming." She handed Jo a bottle of wine.

"Thanks." She stepped back into the hallway. "I was on the phone. Gail called."

Laura's gray eyes studied her own. A smile dimpled her cheeks. "You didn't tell, did you? Neither did I." Laura began looking around, peering into the kitchen, going into the living room. "Nice place!"

"I have you to thank for it." She followed in Gail's wake and switched on the gas fireplace. "What would you like to hear?"

"Whatever you like," Laura said, glancing at the set table in the dining area of the living room.

"Would you like a glass of wine or a mixed drink? All I have is vodka and tonic right now." She switched from public radio to the CD player. The first strains of Bach's double violin concerto filled the room.

"Whatever you're having."

"You're easy to please." She had a bottle of Snoqualmie Sauvignon Blanc cooling in the fridge. Pulling the cork, she poured two glasses and carried them into the living room. "Are you hungry?"

"Moderately. Not starving yet."

They sipped the wine and listened to the music. Outside, street type lamps gave shadowed light to the snow covered lawn leading to the river.

"Where do you live?" Jo asked.

"In an old farmhouse a few miles west of town on a couple of acres. Enough room to let the dog run. He knows the boundaries." Laura turned toward her. "Do you think you're going to like it here?"

"I was kind of lonely over the holiday weekend. I spent every night at Gail's, though she and Connie were gone to Gail's parents. They came back last night, and I stayed then too." She met Laura's solemn gaze with her own. "Partly it was to keep the cat company."

Laura smiled. "Did he appreciate it?"

She grinned back. "He's a feisty little thing. He bit me when I knocked him off the counter."

When they finished their wine, she put water on to boil for the rigatoni. Laura followed her into the kitchen and leaned against a counter.

"Smells good."

"I fixed it yesterday, all except the pasta."

"I cook on the weekends too. I'm usually pretty hungry when I come home after work."

"Aha," Jo said. "You are hungry."

Laura laughed. "Caught in my own words. I'm just making conversation."

"Me too," she admitted. "I'm nervous." Even though the doors were locked, she was afraid Gail might barge in.

Over dinner, she told Laura about her father and mother. "I know you had a great relationship with your mother. How about your father?"

"I loved him. I never knew what to say to him, though," Laura said. "Are you excited about meeting your father."

"In a way I wish we'd never found him. If I like him, I'll be mad because he stayed out of our lives. If I don't like him, I won't want a relationship with him."

"You have a choice anyway." Laura put away a second helping and leaned back in her chair. "Nice table, good food, interesting conversation. Thank you so much."

Now what? Jo decided to let Laura make that decision.

They cleaned up the dishes and returned to the living room, where they took opposite ends of the leather sofa. The lights were turned low, the music rising and falling with each movement. Silence fell between them. Jo drained her glass and set it on the end table.

Laura glanced at her watch. "It's nearly ten. I should go home."

Disappointment washed over Jo. "Already?"

"It'll be ten thirty before I get there. It's been a lovely evening, but I have to let Buddy out."

"I thought . . ." What had she thought?

"Come to my house for dinner Wednesday night." Laura stood and stretched. "Pack a bag."

"What?" she asked, her legs suddenly without strength.

"You can stay over. It'll make for a longer evening. I've got lots of room."

"Wendy never stays overnight during the week?"

"Nope, which is probably why we're still together."

Then she was gone into the chilly night, and Jo phoned Gail. Connie answered.

"I hear you had Mimi over after school."

"Yeah. All she talks about is butthead Bucky. She's boring."

"How's Boo?"

"I think he misses you," the girl said.

Jo laughed. "Yeah, sure. Is your mother around?"

"She's in the bathroom. Boo and I are on her bed." A small silence followed. "Jo, can I see your place sometime? Mom says it's on the river and pretty fancy."

"Sure. Why don't you come for Sunday supper when you get back from your dad's?"

"Mom too?"

"Of course. I thought your hair looked pretty good yesterday, by the way."

"I used a bottle of conditioner on it. Just a sec. Mom's here."

"Close the door, Connie, so the cat doesn't come back in," Gail said. "There's cat hair all over the bed."

"Is there?" Jo asked. "He probably jumped up a time or two."

"You're a softie, Jo."

"Hey, I swept him off the counter twice. He attacked me for it," she said. "You asked me to call you back and here I am."

"Where'd you go tonight?"

"I poked my nose out the door and decided to stay in. I watched a video." She named one she'd seen over the weekend.

"Sure you don't want to move back in with us?"

"I signed the lease and Connie had a friend over today. Oh, by the way, I invited her to have supper here Sunday night. She wants to see the place."

"Can I come too?"

"Of course, silly. She said the cat misses me."
"She misses you."
"Yeah, sure, like she misses taking a test."

Tuesday and Wednesday galloped by, leaving her wondering where the time went. Carol was now calling the clients that Jo and Walter chose to fill requests from area businesses. But the applicants kept coming in, along with calls and e-mail from nearby companies looking for temporary help.

Stopping by the liquor store, she purchased a bottle of chilled champagne and drove the country roads, following Laura's directions. When she crossed over a culvert, she turned into a long driveway that led to a two story farmhouse. A dusk to dawn light lit the space between the garage and the house. There was an outer building with a sagging roof and a barn that had caved in on itself from neglect.

The big dog appeared out of the dusk and raced over the expanse of white yard toward her, ears flattened, tongue lolling.

"Ahhh," she said, falling back into her car and shutting the door. Then she felt foolish. This was Laura's dog. She turned the key and unrolled the window. "Hi, Buddy boy. How are you?"

The dog barked twice and sat down, wagging his long shaggy tail. She would have sworn he was smiling, showing a glimmer of white teeth.

The side door to the house opened and Laura stepped out, arms crossed against the cold. "Buddy, come," she said in a no-nonsense voice. The dog ran toward her. She held his collar while Jo made her way to the door across a broken, narrow sidewalk.

Laura put the champagne in the fridge and led her through a dimly lit dining room with a very large table set for two into the living room. The furnishings were a mix of utilitarian and antique. The dog lay down on a large pad in front of a wood stove and licked its feet.

"Very nice," Jo said, thinking the house a little dark and cramped.

When they returned to the kitchen, Laura popped the cork on the champagne and poured them each a smoking glass. "Did you bring your nightie?"

She had brought an outfit for the next day, along with an overnight bag. She hoped Gail wouldn't phone the condo.

"Come sit down for a few minutes. Dinner's in the oven." Laura led her back to the living room where the dog watched them with soulful eyes from his pad. When Laura sat on the couch, Buddy got to his feet and placed his head in her lap. She buried a hand in his ruff.

Jo took a chair that sank comfortably under her weight. After a couple of minutes, the dog plodded over to her for a pat and a sniff before going back to Laura. "Dinner smells good whatever it is."

"Hope so. I'm experimenting on you. Polenta pie. Got the recipe out of the paper. It's Mexican."

"I love Mexican. Do you like to cook?"

"If I have time, I don't mind."

After dinner, they returned to the living room with cups of decaf. But when Jo started to lower herself into the same chair, Laura patted the cushion beside her on the couch. "Sit here."

Heart pounding, she crossed the oriental carpet to perch uneasily on the sofa. A sudden headache made her blink.

"Are you all right?" Laura asked.

"I shouldn't be doing this. I shouldn't be here."

Laura raised her brows and smiled crookedly. "Nor should I, but we are. Why do you think that's so?"

"You drive me crazy. I can't get that night at the hotel out of my mind." Her breath had shortened. "What do you think?"

"I think we're looking for something, and we'll never find it if we don't allow ourselves some space to search."

"You're experimenting with more than food then?" Jo said with a shaky smile. She might get through this evening without making a fool of herself.

Laura reached for her hand and held it between her own. "I want you."

She let herself be led into a small bedroom off the living room, where the small bedlamp cast a soft light. Then she stood shivering while Laura undressed her, folding each item and placing it on top of the others in a neat pile on a small rocking chair. Laura removed her own clothes and pulled Jo backwards to the double bed.

The quilts buried them under their weight and volume. Outside, trees creaked in the gusting wind. The dog padded into the room and curled with a thump on the rug next to the bed.

Laura's hand moved gently over her. "You are so luscious. Do you know that?"

"A little fleshy," she said with a nervous laugh.

"I love it." Laura sought out Jo's mouth with her lips. "Promise me you won't lose any weight?"

"I want to look the way you do, trim and athletic, not like a Flemish painting."

Laura's throaty laugh raised the hair on the back of Jo's neck. "I like you just the way you are."

Jo rolled on top of Laura and, supporting her weight with her arms, looked down at her. Her skin tingled as Laura's fingers twined in her hair and moved over her back. She slipped off to the side, facing Laura.

The ringing phone brought them both to sitting positions, where they waited in rigid silence for the answering machine to kick in.

"It's me. Nothing important. Just wanted to talk. I'll catch you tomorrow. Love you."

Jo took a deep breath. "Wendy?"

"Yes. Sorry." Laura lay back and pulled on Jo's arm.

"I can't," Jo said.

"Lie down next to me."

After a while, Jo fell asleep. Sometime in the night she wakened to Laura's touch. Pretending sleep, she lay quietly while the hand caressed her breasts and midriff. When it stole between her legs, she turned toward Laura and pulled her close.

XIX

She woke disoriented, before realizing where she was and with whom. Laura's back was turned to her. Listening to nothing more than the house creaking, the furnace kicking in, the dog licking himself, she wished she could have this day with Laura. She longed to make love again in the light of day and began to dwell on the previous night.

Laura turned over and nestled into Jo's shoulder within the shelter of her arm. "Morning," she said hoarsely. "Sleep well?"

"So well I didn't know where I was when I woke up."

The radio came on then, informing them that it was six twenty-nine on a cold, sunny day with temperatures predicted in the thirties.

"Where did you spend Thanksgiving?"

"Here with friends," Laura said, stretching and peering up at her. "Why?"

"Just curious. I'll never see you on holidays."

"I'll never see you on weekends." Laura swallowed a yawn and worked her way out of bed.

Jo sat up and threw her legs over the side of the mattress. She was desperate to pee.

"Here." Laura grinned and threw her a long terry cloth bathrobe. "Put this on."

Her face in the mirror looked back at her, mouth swollen, eyelids drooping, one side creased. She remembered her clothes and overnight bag left in the car. Dashing outside in the bathrobe and Laura's boots she fetched her things.

Over toast and coffee, she met Laura's gray gaze somberly. "Where is this going?"

"Wherever we want it to," Laura replied, giving a crust to the waiting dog. "You look nice."

She wore a black pinstriped suit and a white blouse. Low heels completed the outfit. "Thanks."

"I wear jeans or chinos mostly. I draw the line with shorts, though. There's always the white jacket to cover me up."

"You'd look good in anything," Jo remarked. "Can you spend Monday night at my place?"

"I can't leave Buddy alone all night. You come here. Mondays and Wednesdays. How does that sound?"

"Sounds like I won't be home much." At least, she wouldn't be lonely or bored.

There was a message from Gail on her voice mail at work. "Where are you?"

She called Gail at her job, got her voice mail, and left a

message for her. "I went shopping but didn't feel good, so I went home to bed. I never heard the phone."

Cramps bound her into a knot. She gasped and sat down, her arms wrapped around her middle. That's how Walter found her when he knocked on the partly open door and walked in.

"What's the matter, Jo?" He set the cups down and dashed around the desk.

She would have laughed if she hadn't been bent over with pain. If this is what cheating did to her, she better give it up. "Don't know," she muttered through her teeth.

"I'll take you home," he said.

"No, no. I've got too much to do. Just give me a few minutes." But was it cheating? Was she committed to Gail now that they were separated? She felt a little better and tentatively straightened up and took a deep breath. No pain. Good. "There. I'm better." She smiled at him and felt something loosening. "Oops. I'll be right back."

Diarrhea. What caused it? The polenta pie? Gail's phone call? Her affair with Laura? Flu? She sat long enough so that Walter was talking to Carol at the front desk when she got back. Her legs trembled.

"You look ghastly," Walter said. "You really must go home."

"Thanks," she said, "but I'm okay now."

"I'm right out here if you need something," Carol said.

The two people in the waiting room looked up at her, and she groaned. One of them was Keith Csyzka, still needing a shave. "Didn't we find you a job? Aren't you filling in for one of the cheese factories?"

"Yeah, but they put me on full time. I don't want no full time."

"Why not?" Walter asked, hitching up the slacks that hung below his belly.

"I had to get up at four in the morning. I couldn't do that."

"Why not?" Walter insisted.

"Find me something where I don't have to get up so damn early."

"You're lucky to get any work," Walter said.

"I told the lady what I wanted." Csyzka looked and sounded on edge. He stood up, taller and more muscular than Walter.

Walter said, "We'll call you if something else comes up."

Csyzka's jaw muscles tightened. If there hadn't been so much other noise, they'd have heard his teeth grinding. "You give me that job on purpose, didn't you?"

Jo had. "I thought it was a good fit."

Walter waved him toward the door. "We'll call you," he said.

Jo had forgotten about her intestines in the tenseness of the moment. Then she was gripped with another bout and fled for the women's room. After that, she went home.

It was there that Gail finally got hold of her as the bedroom darkened toward late afternoon. "Carol said you left work sick."

"Yep. The dreaded diarrhea." She craved only water which she sipped in small quantities.

"I came by the condo last night when I couldn't get hold of you."

"Don't do that, Gail. Don't check up on me," she said with anger.

"I was worried. I couldn't raise you."

"I was either shopping or in bed. I didn't know you were here."

"Are you coming over tomorrow night?"

"Why don't you come here overnight?"

"The cat . . ." Gail began.

"Cats, dogs. I'll never get to stay here," she blurted her frustration.

"What are you talking about?"

"Nothing. I'll be there after work. Do you want to go out to eat?"

"We'll play it by ear. Get well."

"Wait a minute. Are you going with Kim and me on Saturday?"

"I think I'll stay home this time."

Good, she thought. She wanted to talk privately to her sister. They'd agreed to meet at Kim's around nine in the morning.

Saturday a cool sun shone on wet streets and white snow. An inch had fallen the night before.

Jo had a cup of coffee with Kim and Brad before they left. The little kids were watching cartoons. The oldest two were still in bed. Kim kissed Brad good-bye and followed her out the door.

On the road, she asked, "Did cheating on Brad make you physically sick?"

"I only cheated that one weekend. It made me nervous, not ill. Why?"

"I spent Wednesday night with Laura and had to go home from work Thursday. My guts were in tangles."

"If it happens again, maybe you could consider the cheating as the cause. Otherwise, no. I read somewhere that cheating confuses the issues. It doesn't clear them up. The one you're cheating with always looks better than the one you're living with, because you don't have the constant contact that causes friction." Kim put a hand across the back of Jo's seat and tugged on her hair. "So stop it already."

"I can't seem to do that. Not yet. Besides, I'm not living with either one. Do you think I'm looking for something?"

"I think you're going to find a whole lotta heartache. Cheating blows a huge hole in a relationship. When the trust is gone, so is everything else. That's why I'll never tell Brad about that weekend."

"Do you think Brad has had any affairs?"

"Yeah. I do. But I don't ask, because I don't want to know."

"Right now?"

"I don't think so, but who knows."

They drove in silence for a while before Jo admitted, "I'm nervous."

"Me too. I don't know why, though. We've lived all these years without a real father."

Driving into Milwaukee on Hwy 94, they exited downtown and followed the directions north to the bookstore tucked among three other small businesses near a corner. Twice they drove around the block, looking for an empty parking spot. The cars crammed nose to tail along the curbs left little space for two cars to pass. Finally, they wriggled into a parking spot as someone pulled out.

The wind tunneled down the street, whipping their hair, causing them to hunker into their jackets. They arrived at the front door of The Written Word, climbed the steps, and stood for a moment in the shelter of the doorway before Kim pushed inside.

The building was old with high ceilings and dangling flourescent lights and fans. Bookshelves divided the interior into narrow aisles, making it seem cramped. Near the front were new books. The two women peered at the titles, most of which had gay and lesbian content. On one rack stood gay magazines and calendars. Tacked to the wall hung announcements of meetings and concerts.

He came up behind them, making them both jump when he spoke. "Do you need any help?"

They turned together and stared at him — a tall, stooped, skinny man with dark sunken eyes and thick, unruly gray hair. He smiled a little. "Are you who I think you are?"

Kim pulled herself together first. She nodded. "I'm Kim. This is Jo. I suppose she's your namesake."

He looked at Jo with sad eyes. "I'm surprised your mother didn't change your name."

Jo found her voice. "So am I. Probably too much bother."

"Come on. I've got coffee brewing and sandwiches from the corner deli. Are you hungry?" He started toward the center of the store where a counter encircled a check-out area.

They both chose tuna on rye with chips and carried them with cups of decaf to fold-out chairs.

Kim took a bite and said, "It's good."

He sat on the edge of the desk and crossed his arms. "Tell me about yourselves."

Jo shifted in the padded seat and swallowed the bite she'd taken of the tuna on rye. "You first," she said to Kim.

Hearing Kim's summary of her life as she saw it, watching this man listen almost hungrily, made the anger in her bubble to the surface. When Kim was silent, she said, "You could have been a part of it."

He studied her for a moment while she returned his sad stare with her angry one. Then he sighed. "You have to understand what it was like back then, what I was like, what your mother was like. I took the easy way out. I'm not proud of that." A distant look came into his eyes. "I remember watching you two in the park where your baby sitter took you. But then your mother saw me there and when I went back, you were never there again. When she remarried, I let you go." The side of his mouth pulled up in a wry smile. "I really have no excuses."

"Let it go, Jo," Kim said. "It doesn't matter now."

"I'm sorry," he added.

Jo shrugged.

"How about you? Are you with someone?" he asked.

"Are you?" she rebutted.

"Yes. Would you like to meet him?"

"Sure," Kim said.

He picked up the phone and summoned his roommate downstairs. "We live on the second floor. Very economical and handy. I'm not a rich man."

"We weren't looking for money," Jo said.

Kim added, "We wanted to meet you."

"Before we died or you did," Jo added.

He laughed, a rich sound that surprised Jo with its humor. "I didn't think you were looking for money. I guess I was excusing my lack of success in that area. I'm a little left of center."

"So are we," Kim assured him.

The man who approached from the rear of the store was short, also graying, but very fit. His brown eyes sparked with life and humor. He thrust out a hand. "I'm Thomas."

"Kim and Jo, my daughters," their father said with a smile.

"You must stay for dinner," Thomas said. "I'm cooking up a storm. Somebody has to eat it."

Jo started to shake her head, but Kim said, "We'd love to." Jo glared at her.

They spent the afternoon talking to both men and exploring the books in the store. The people who came and went were mostly interested in the gay and lesbian material. Joe sometimes introduced Kim and Jo as his daughters, and they were greeted with surprise and warmth.

Kim called home first to say they would be late, then Jo phoned Gail who asked, "What's he like?"

"I'll tell you when I get back." After hanging up, she turned to Kim and whispered, "We're not staying overnight, no matter what."

"I've got five kids waiting. I'm the one who has to go home."

"When am I going to meet these five kids?" Joe asked.

"When are you coming to visit? Both of you," Kim said.

"We can't both come. We're open seven days a week," Thomas replied.

"Get someone else to work." Kim was not easily dissuaded. "How about Christmas?"

Thomas admitted he loved to cook when she and Kim praised the homemade refried beans and Spanish rice, the chicken burritos, the taco salad. Determined to drive home that evening, Jo only drank one margarita.

Joe studied the two women with a soft light in his eyes. He lifted what must have been his third margarita. "I can't believe you're here. You're living testimony that sometimes what you wish comes true and sometimes it's better than you thought it would be."

Patting Joe on the back, Thomas said, "Liquor makes him sentimental, but what he said is true. He's often spoke of wanting to know you. It's unreal that you're here."

"It's real enough." Jo couldn't resist. "You don't ask and expect to receive. You go out and get it."

"I know," Thomas replied with a smile, "but Joe is not one to impose himself where he's not wanted."

"Who said he wasn't wanted? No one asked us."

No one said anything for a moment, then Thomas broke the silence with a joke.

XX

Driving home through a vortex of snowflakes, Jo demanded, “Well?”

“Well, what? Weren’t you pleased? I loved them both.”

“Equally, right? Do you feel any daughterly affection?”

“What I feel is enough for now. Come on, Jo. Did you know you were so angry?”

She felt as if the breath had been knocked out of her. “No. It surprised me.” She thought about that awhile before saying, “I probably do remember him.”

“Maybe that’s why. You remember his leaving. I don’t.”

It was after eleven when she dropped Kim off at her house. The motion lights lit her sister’s way inside. She waited till the door closed behind her before she turned the car toward Gail's house.

Letting herself in the side door, she was greeted by the meowing cat. Bending over, she stroked the gray coat. "Hey furball, how was your day? Why aren't you in bed?"

She looked up, startled. Gail was standing in the doorway, wrapped in her bathrobe. "Dumb cat never answers," she remarked sheepishly.

"Come to bed," Gail said.

Following Gail up the stairs, she piled her clothes on a chair on her side of the bed and climbed under the covers. "It's snowing."

"I know. I was worried." Gail threw an arm over her. "Tell me everything. What he looks like, where he lives, what the store is like, who he's with. Don't leave anything out."

She complied. Her voice sounded disembodied in the dark room. The cat meowed outside the door, while the snow hissed against the window. Drowsiness slurred her voice about the time she realized Gail had fallen asleep. She let herself follow.

They talked all the next day, up till the time Jo went to the condo to fix supper. Gail would follow with Connie when she got home.

Jo fixed Connie's favorite meal — pizza. She'd bought a couple of crusts, tomatoes for sauce, cheese, basil, and broccoli for toppings. As the tomatoes simmered, she grated the cheese and washed and cut up the broccoli. Lastly, she made up an hors d'oeuvre plate of a cheese spread and crackers. She had bought Connie's favorite root beer and a red wine for herself and Gail.

Putting another selection of CD's on the turntable — a Carmen suite, Groffe's *Grand Canyon Suite,* a CD of Andrew Lloyd Webber tunes, Dave Brubeck's *Take Five,* one with a mix of classical including Barber's *Adagio for Strings,* and a Sheryl Crow of her own. She had no idea whether Connie would like the music but told herself she'd tried. Next she turned on the gas fireplace and the table lamps before setting the dining table for three.

When she heard the doorbell, she switched the receiver from radio to CD and hurried to open up. Connie stood slightly behind her mother on the door step. In the entryway, Jo took their jackets.

"How was your weekend?" she asked the girl

"Okay." The girl followed her mother into the living room and gazed around in awe. "Holy cow! No wonder you moved out of our house."

Jo came up behind her and took in the room as she must see it. "That's not why I moved out. You are why I moved out. I wanted to give you back your space."

"Aren't you the martyr?" Connie said.

"Look. You wanted to see the place. Quit insulting me and go sit down with your mother. Enjoy the view."

Silenced, Connie joined her mother on the leather sofa. Jo heard her exclamations about how soft it was. "Somebody must have chewed the leather."

Jo laughed, then poured the wine and root beer and carried the glasses into the living room on a tray along with the cheese spread and cracker plate. Setting them down on the coffee table, she took her glass to one of the leather chairs.

"Fancy, schmancy," the girl said, spreading a cracker and popping it in her mouth.

Jo felt herself being molded into the leather. "I try," she said with a twist of smile. "How are Mimi and Butthead?" The Carmen suite flowed through her, loosening her joints.

"I think they're suited for each other," Connie remarked. "Have a cracker, Mom, before I eat them all."

"I will," Gail said. "You know, Connie, you'd have an easier time of it if you could learn to curb your tongue."

"What fun would that be?" Jo said. Outside the plate glass windows, the yard lights cast shadows across the snow.

"Can I see the rest of the place?" Connie asked.

"Be my guest." Jo swept an arm toward the bedrooms and

watched the girl disappear down the hall. "She's in her usual tart form."

"I'm sorry. I don't know what gets into her."

"Don't be. She's as feisty as the cat. No boy is going to walk over her."

Connie reappeared, heading for the kitchen and the downstairs. A few minutes later she was back, finishing off the crackers.

"Want more?" Jo asked.

"Don't let her spoil her appetite," her mother chided.

"I won't. It's pizza." The girl looked at Jo. "I liked the James Herriot book."

Surprised and pleased, Jo said, "Good. I almost forgot. I bought you another in the series at my father's bookstore." She went to the bedroom to get it.

Connie took the book and stared at the cover. "Thanks."

"Open it," Jo urged. Inside she had written the date and inscribed: Connie, The gift of a book needs no special occasion. Fondly, Jo.

Connie said nothing, only chewed harder on her lip and swallowed a couple of times. Without a word, she got up and went to the nearest bathroom.

Gail picked up the book and read the inscription, then looked at Jo. "I'll bet she's in there crying."

"I didn't mean to make her cry. I gave you a book, too."

"Yes and you wrote, 'From my father's house to yours, my love.' I teared some, too."

"I'm going to fix the pizzas. Want to help?"

Connie ate most of one pizza, devouring it with hardly a word in between bites. She, too, wanted to hear about Jo's meeting with her father.

"I didn't want to like him, but I did," she said. "He deserted us and we're going to forgive him."

"Yeah? I'd tell him to eff off," Connie remarked.

"Connie," her mother warned.

"Can we spend a night here sometime?" the girl asked.

"No pets," Jo said. "You'd have to leave Boo at home."

"He'd be okay one night."

When they left, Gail kissed Jo on the cheek and whispered, "It doesn't feel right leaving you here."

"I know." It didn't. "See you Friday."

The attorney called at work the next day. Jo had suggested she tell Mark to send the divorce papers to her office along with a financial statement. "There's a lot of money here. The house and grounds, your retirements and investments. I want you to look this over."

She dropped into Audrey Compton's office and perused the statements of their joint holdings. It was Mark who had handled the finances. Most of the purchases had been made out of his salary. They had used hers for day to day expenses. She licked her lips. "I have to think about this. Most of these investments were made by Mark, not me."

At the condo, she set the statements on the bedside table to study over the next day, then phoned Gail. She had to somehow head off any phone calls from Gail that night. Hiding an affair was more complicated with Gail than it had been with Mark.

Connie answered. "Mom's not home."

"Why not?" she asked.

"It's not my day to watch her," Connie said. "I started the book you gave me last night."

"Do you like it?"

"Yeah. Want to say hello to Boo?" A faint meow reached Jo's ear.

"Tell your mom I'm going to be gone tonight."

"Did you hear him?" the girl asked.

"Yes, I heard him. Did you hear me?"

"I'll tell her, but she said she's going to be late. She's going out with friends."

"She didn't say anything about going anywhere last night," Jo complained.

"She says she's getting forgetful."

"Let it go then. Don't tell her."

"Don't be mad at me," the girl said.

"I'm not. What are you going to do?"

"Throw a party. What do you think? Study, read. I lead a boring life. I gotta go. Someone's at the door."

"Maybe you shouldn't open the door if you're alone," Jo warned.

"It's just James, my funny friend. Don't worry. James is a lot like you and Mom."

By the time she left for Laura's, she was worried. Where was Gail and with whom? And did Gail know her daughter was alone in the house with this boy?

Knowing she would be late, she swung by Connie's house, parking out front. Heading up the walkway, she unlocked the door with her own key, then knocked and went inside.

Two young faces looked up from the dining table with alarm. The boy jumped to his feet but appeared uncertain what to do next.

"Sit down, James. It's just my stepmother two. What are you doing here? Checking up on me?"

"I guess you could say that." She gave a shrug, rattled by the stepmother two title.

"You don't live here anymore."

"That doesn't mean I don't worry."

"James isn't about to attack me or anything, are you James?"

The boy's face turned a deep red. He stammered a no.

Jo smiled, stepped forward, and stretched out a hand. "I'm Jo, James. Maybe I worry too much." Only then did she notice the cat, which was meowing for her attention. Bending down, she stroked him absently. “I better go.”

She parked in front of Laura’s garage and hurried to the back door. The dog barked on the other side and Laura opened to let her in.

“Sorry I’m late,” she said, patting the dog while ascending the few steps to the brightly lit kitchen.

Laura wore jeans and sweatshirt. There were no enticing smells in the air. “I thought maybe you got hung up with something.”

“I took a detour by Gail’s house to check up on Connie. She was alone with this boy. I know I shouldn’t have shown such a lack of trust. He seemed a nice enough kid.”

“The nicest kids still contend with raging hormones.”

“I think his hormones are directed toward other boys,” she said. “Can I help with something?”

“I thought I’d treat you to dinner out at the nearby supper club. It’s your basic fare and not very good at that, but I ran short on time. What do you say?”

“Sounds good as long as I pay my own way.”

Laura shrugged. “Let me get my coat.”

“I’ll drive,” Jo said.

Pete and Mary’s Supper Club was located on a busy corner. Jo found an empty slot and pulled in between two SUV’s that dwarfed her Sebring. Slinging her purse over her shoulder she followed Laura into the smoky, dark interior.

They took a table in the long room behind the bar. Jo ordered a vodka and tonic and studied the dinner choices.

“The prime rib is probably the best thing on the menu,” Laura said, sipping a glass of white wine.

“I’ve got a yen for a burger and fries.” She closed the menu and looked around. The place was half full. “Do you know any of these people?”

“Sure.” Laura lifted her chin and smiled at a couple a few tables away. “I vet their dairy herd. Nice people.” She turned to Jo. “So how was your meeting with your father?”

"It went off better than I thought. What surprised me was the anger I felt toward him for disappearing from our lives. Kim and I grew up with a mother who mostly ignored us and a stepfather who tolerated us. He might have made a difference."

"How does Kim feel?" Laura's gray eyes squinted in the smoky air.

"She's ready to forgive and forget."

Laura waved at someone across the room. "You might as well, too."

"I guess," she said. Agreeing did nothing to change the injustice she felt at being abandoned.

When they bounced down Laura's driveway, Jo had second thoughts about staying the night, but Laura dispensed with those by grabbing her bag and taking it inside.

Already a little weak kneed with expectation, Jo carried the hanging clothes inside.

Laura put Jo's overnight case in the bedroom, turned on the bed lamp, and returned to the living room. "Take a load off. Want a glass of wine or something?"

Jo shook her head, her heart pounding hard enough to affect her breathing.

Laura sat next to Jo, tucking a leg under her. She gave Jo a wicked smile and a searching look before leaning in to kiss her and slide a hand down her jeans.

They sprang apart guiltily when the phone rang into the otherwise silent room. Laura's eyes darkened and she licked her lips as she got up to answer.

"Hi. How's it going?" She listened. "Of course, I do. I would have called but there's not much news at this end." More listening. "Me too. I'll pick you up at the airport on Friday. Tell the pilot to drive carefully." Hanging up, she smiled at Jo and crossed the room to sit next to her. "Sorry about that. Wendy travels for one of the paper companies. She's in Cleveland."

"It's okay," Jo said. She wasn't proud of her behavior. Now

would be a good time to end it, to try to make this just a friendship. Instead, she found herself responding to Laura's advances with her own.

When they made the move from couch to bed, undressing each other quickly and burrowing under the covers in an embrace, Jo thought, Too late to turn back now.

Sometime in the night she wakened to Laura's touch. As before, she lay quietly pretending sleep while Laura's hand moved over her. Only when thoroughly aroused did she respond by rolling on top of Laura.

The next morning the radio brought her to a disorienting semi-conscious state. Glancing over, as Laura scooted over to lie within the circle of her arm, she asked, "Sleep well?"

"Yes. Did you?"

"Yeah. It's like a cave in here at night."

The dog scrambled to his feet and laid his long nose on the comforter. Laura reached over Jo and scratched behind his ears. "Do you have to go out, Bud?"

Buddy whined and wagged his tail.

"Guess that means yes," Laura said, working her way to the other side of the bed. "Stay there. I'll turn up the heat and be right back."

Jo lifted the blinds on the window nearest the bed. Snow had fallen during the night. The trees and bushes and her car were covered in a layer of dazzling white crystals. She saw the dog frolicking in the snow, throwing it up in the air with his nose.

Laura slid back under the covers and snuggled close. "Being a vet in the winter, the kind who visits farms, is not always fun."

"I'll bet," Jo said. "What are you in for today?"

"I have to worm a bunch of horses."

"Dress warm."

Laura pulled coveralls over jeans and a hooded sweatshirt before going out the door. "I really like you," she declared, giving Jo a big kiss.

"I hope so, considering what we're doing," Jo replied with raised brows. "What happens if we blow everything up?"

"You mean Gail and Wendy?" Laura asked. When Jo nodded, she said, "Are you worried about that?"

They were walking through the few inches of snow. "Well, yeah, aren't you?"

"Kind of."

"Maybe we should just be friends," Jo suggested.

Laura laughed. "A little late for that, isn't it?"

They had reached the garage, and Laura opened the doors. Buddy jumped into the front seat, leaving a trail of snow. "See you on Wednesday?"

"I don't know. I'll call you." Jo brushed the fluffy snow off her car before getting inside.

XXI

On the drive to work, Jo imagined potential conversations in which she would level with Gail:

"Gail, I've been seeing Laura twice a week."

"Seeing her in what way?" Gail would ask.

"I've been spending nights there."

"You can't be with both of us, Jo. Make a choice."

And there she'd be, having to give up Gail when Laura might not give up Wendy. She found herself thinking about Connie and how she would respond to her infidelity.

"I always knew you were a pervert," Connie would say.

How would she deny it, and why did she care? Betraying Gail was akin to betraying her daughter. Connie'd never understand. She'd simply judge her.

At work, she hung up her coat and set her purse in her desk drawer after walking through the empty waiting room. The front door was unlocked. Carol must be in the women's room. She would await her return to go there herself. Starting the coffee, she turned on her computer and logged onto e-mail.

Sensing someone at the door, she looked up as Walter took a seat in front of her desk. "Have you seen Carol?" he asked.

"I think I'll check the bathroom," she said, uneasy now.

"I'll wait here."

She pushed open the door to the women's room with difficulty, peering around it to see why it was so heavy.

Carol leaned against it, legs spraddled, hair disheveled, cheeks unnaturally red, lip split, the white teeth stained with blood.

"What the hell," she said with alarm, working her way through thc narrow opening, and supporting Carol. "What happened?"

"Keith Csyzka," Carol said. "He was waiting when I got here. He tried to . . ." She shuddered, her eyes terrified. "He's gone, isn't he? He said he'd hurt me if I told anyone."

"I didn't see him." Jo led the other woman to the lone chair in the bathroom and sat her down. "Let me clean you up a little, then we'll call the police. They'll track him down."

"I'm scared, Jo. They won't keep him off the street long." Her eyes pleaded with Jo, who felt her hair prickle on the back of her neck.

Wetting a paper towel, she dabbed at Carol's face rather ineffectually. "I'm going to get Walter. Okay?"

"I'll come with you." Carol got shakily to her feet. "Don't leave me here."

Half supporting Carol, they made their way past curious looks in the waiting room to Jo's office.

Walter set the coffee pot down carefully as they limped through the door. "What the hell . . ."

"Keith Csyzka did this. Will you call the police?" Jo sat Carol down in the chair Walter had vacated. She closed the door to the waiting room and jerked her head at it. "What do we do with them?"

"I'll ask them to return tomorrow," Walter said.

Carol brushed at her wrinkled skirt. "I kicked him in the shins a couple of times and he just kept coming."

Walter and Jo exchanged glances.

"Not coming like that," Carol said. "He wouldn't let me up. He sure made a mess of my clothes." She tried a smile which ran off her face to be replaced by tears. "Then we heard someone's footsteps. It must have been you, Jo."

"I should have gone to the john, instead of waiting for you to come out."

Walter hung up after talking to the police. "They're on their way. Want some coffee, Carol?"

Carol nodded, but the cup shook so badly in her hands that she had to put it down.

When someone tapped on the door, they turned expecting the police. Instead, Mark stood in the entrance. Caught off guard, Jo frowned at him.

Mark took a step into the room, nodding at Walter and looking with hesitation at Carol. "What happened here?"

"A little matter of assault," Jo said. "More to the point, why are you here?"

Mark glanced at her and then back at Carol with concern. "The divorce papers and financial disclosure, Jo, you haven't responded." He waved a hand. "Can I help?"

There was another knock and two police officers joined them — a thirty some woman and an older man. They refused Walter's offer of coffee and questioned Carol about the assault. Standing near the door, Jo failed to hear most of what Carol said.

It was Jo who went to the hospital with Carol and took

her home to her apartment. Terrified of being left alone, Carol begged Jo to stay until a friend came to take her place.

Returning to the office, she found Walter sitting at the reception desk, answering incoming phone calls. He looked up. "How is she?"

"Scared to death. That son of a bitch, I knew he was bad news. Have the police picked him up yet?"

"I don't know," Walter said, studying her. "You and Mark are divorcing?"

She shuffled her feet. "I didn't want to talk about it, Walter."

"I understand," he said. "I didn't either when I separated from my wife."

"It's just too complicated."

"Hey, it's okay."

"I'll stay out here," she volunteered.

"Thanks. I think we'll convert the storage room into an office for Carol and hire someone else, maybe some of our temps. She won't want to work out here anymore."

"It happened in the bathroom," Jo pointed out.

"That's true. We'll let her decide."

At the condo that evening, she poured herself a vodka and tonic. She rarely drank during the week, almost never when she was alone. She gulped down the liquor as if dying of thirst. When the phone rang, she sunk further into gloom and made no move to answer until Gail's voice came on the answering machine. Then she picked up.

"Are you screening your calls?" Gail asked.

"Let's just say it was a bad day." She told her what happened.

"Sounds like Carol had a worse one. You better not go into the john alone."

"I can't take Walter with me," she said. "I should call Carol and see how she is."

"Connie said you checked up on her last night. Sweet of you."

"Did you know she was with this James?"

"I think she did mention it in passing."

"How was your evening out with friends?" Jo asked.

"Okay. We went out to eat and to the movies. It's not the same as being with you, but I have to keep moving forward," Gail said.

"What the hell does that mean?"

"I'm not going to sit around the house, waiting for you to show up. Where were you when I called at ten thirty last night?"

"Probably in bed," Jo lied.

Carol let the answering machine pick up before she answered too. "Hi, Jo."

"Are you alone?"

"No. My friend's spending the night." Carol sounded more upbeat. "Mark has been very helpful. He's the one who suggested I let the answering machine tell me who was on the line." She added, "I hope you don't mind."

"I have nothing to say about what he does anymore. We're getting a divorce," Jo said. But she did mind, which suprised her.

"He phoned to ask how I was. So did Walter, of course. I thought you must have given Mark my number."

"Nope. Maybe he asked Walter, but he is an attorney. He has ways of finding things out."

"You really don't mind, Jo? I wouldn't do anything to offend you."

"Of course not."

She hung up feeling even more glum and poured herself another drink. After watching a program on public television, she took her book to bed and fell asleep with it on her chest.

The next day she and Walter played catch-up. Carol came in late and took over the reception desk. When Walter offered her an office, she said she could work from where she was. It was more public, more safe.

At the end of the afternoon, she realized she hadn't called Laura as she'd promised. Nor had Laura phoned her.

Stopping at the grocery store, she picked up milk, bread, a salmon fillet, brocolli, and red potatoes. She'd stay home, cook herself a good meal, and finish her book.

She was broiling the salmon, steaming the brocolli and red potatoes when the doorbell rang. Turning on the outer light, she peered through the small pane of glass. Csyzka's attack on Carol had spooked her. It was Laura.

Opening the door, she said, "You're just in time for dinner."

Laura wiped her feet on the entry rug. "I just got off work and decided to stop by on my way home. We never decided who was going where."

"Sorry I didn't call. It's been a busy two days. I've got to check the salmon. Come on in the kitchen." She'd bought enough just in case Laura showed up.

While they ate in the kitchen at the counter, Jo told her about Carol.

"Have they found this guy?"

"Nope, not last I heard." If it made Jo nervous knowing he was on the loose, it must terrify Carol. "How was the worming Monday?"

"One of the mares at this place rears and strikes. We weren't quick enough. She grazed my shoulder. I'll have to show it to you."

She supposed that meant they'd be in bed before long and murmured, "Dangerous occupation."

"There weren't any assaulters in the stable bathroom," Laura said.

Jo tried to imagine Laura at work. "How do you worm a horse?"

"The hard part is getting the tube up the nose and down to the stomach. Pouring the solution in is easy."

"How do you get a horse to stand still for that?"

"You twitch them. Want to come along Saturday morning? I'm going to one of the biggest stables around."

"Sure." How would she explain it to Gail? "Can I bring Connie. She's reading James Herriot's books."

"By all means. Bring Gail if you want."

"Why don't you ask Wendy, too? We'll all go."

A smile played across Laura's face. "Do I hear a little sarcasm?"

"Don't you ever struggle with guilt?"

"Of course. But as the saying goes, if I can't take the heat, I better get out of the kitchen."

At ten Laura got up out of the warm bed and pulled on her clothes. "That was nice. Are you going to walk me to the door?"

Jo sighed.

When Laura was gone, she returned to the bed and tossed a long time before falling asleep. Gail never called.

Friday she picked up a bottle of wine before driving to Gail's. She had phoned her Thursday evening to ask if she and Connie wanted to go to the stable with her on Saturday. Gail had put Connie on the line.

"Can James come too?" Connie asked.

"I don't care."

"I'll stay home Friday night then."

As she bounced into the driveway and parked under the overhang, she found herself looking forward to seeing not only Gail but Connie, too. Unlocking the side door, she let herself into the house. It's familiarity closed around her in a friendly fashion. As she stood in the kitchen listening to the thump of

Connie's music overhead, she felt the tension of the week draining out of her. The clock ticked, the fridge hummed.

Walking through the empty downstairs, she ran a hand over the worn furniture before climbing the steps to the second floor. Knocking on Connie's door, she called, "Hey girl, are you torturing Boo with that music?"

The door cracked open a bit and Connie's face appeared. "You can have him. He's under the bed." She reached behind her and pushed the animal out the door.

"Hi, James," Jo called on a hunch.

"We're doing homework," Connie said, her face flushing, "and how did you know he was here?"

"Maybe you better do your homework downstairs. Your mother will be home soon." She picked up the mewling cat and took him to the other bedroom to change clothes.

When she got downstairs, Connie was slouched on a chair, arms crossed, in an obvious fit of pique. "You're not my mother, you know."

"Where's James?"

"He went home. What do you think? We're working on a project. Now he probably won't come tomorrow."

She studied the girl, the furrowed brows, the sullen mouth. "What were you doing up there anyway when your mother and I were due home any minute?"

"Mom knows he's just a friend. His hero is a basketball star and not a girl, for God's sake."

"She knows you do your homework in your room?" She didn't want to hassle the kid.

"Yeah. He's gay. The kids tease him about it." The blue eyes flashed in her direction.

XXII

The next morning James showed up at nine as the three of them finished a relatively silent breakfast. On the drive, when startled by Connie's laughter, Jo glanced in the rearview mirror to see James miming some opera singer on the Classics by Request program on public radio. Connie lit up when she laughed, her expression so different from the deadpan she'd perfected. At the sight of James' long arms flung out, his mouth wide, she laughed too. Gail turned to look but realizing he was discovered, James dropped the act.

Weatherby Stables, a white steel barn, was positioned at the end of a long, gravel driveway laced with potholes. Jo parked her car next to Laura's truck in front of the barn,

Buddy sat behind the wheel. He grinned at Jo, his ears bobbing up and down in a silent greeting. She grinned back foolishly.

"You know the dog, too?" Gail asked.

"He accompanies her everywhere, including the clinic."

"He does, Mom," Connie said. She was dressed in torn jeans and a too large sweatshirt and jacket.

Hunching in her coat, Jo opened the door to the stable and stepped inside. It was cold and damp and smelled of hay. She walked around a large riding arena with Gail beside her, Connie and James following, toward the sound of voices.

Just beyond the riding arena was a wash rack and grooming area opposite a tack room, the door open to reveal saddles on racks and bridles on pegs. Beyond these were the stalls on either side of the hard packed dirt aisle. Dust motes danced in the streaked light that filtered through dusty windows and skylights.

Horses hung their long necks and heads over their stall doors, softly nickering. Except for color and size, they all looked pretty much alike to Jo. One snorted as she passed its stall. She jumped.

Laura was bathed in light from open double doors. With her were a beefy man and a slender woman. Between them a horse stood quietly, the rings of its halter fastened on each side to nylon ropes that hung from two by fours on either side of the aisle.

The guilt hit Jo. What had she been thinking, inviting Gail along? It was like a double betrayal to bring her here where Laura was working. Awkwardness made her stammer a hello. Gail glanced curiously at her.

"I hope you don't mind. They wanted to watch a horse being wormed. It's so hard to explain," Laura said after greeting Jo and Gail and introducing them to the owners of the stable, Mac and Dottie. Connie and James, who had stopped to stroke horses' muzzles at each stall, were halfway down the aisle.

"Not at all," Dottie said in a booming voice that belied her small size. "Glad to have you."

Mac grinned and spit a brown stream toward the door. "It ain't what I'd choose to do on a cold morning if I had any choice."

Speaking softly to the horse, Laura took hold of its nose, put a small circle of rope around it and twisted it tight with its two foot handle, then handed that end to the man. The horse stretched its nose out and wiggled it. It stood dociley with mouth open, legs spraddled, eyes nearly closed, penis dropped. Jo looked on with horror.

"Twitching doesn't hurt," Laura assured them. "While the horse concentrates on breathing, we get the worming done. It's a way to pacify the animal without shots."

She then pulled a tube out of a pail of water and inserted it in the horse's nostril and slowly shoved the length of it down the animal's throat. Jo could see the horse swallowing and Laura feeling the progression of the tube down the long neck. Holding one end of the tube in the air, Laura put a funnel in the tube, reached for the plastic container hanging on the bucket, and poured its contents down the tube.

After Laura pulled the tube carefully out of the horse's throat, the man untwisted the twitch. The horse wriggled its nose while Dottie rubbed it. When the animal blew and shook, Jo and Gail stepped back in alarm.

"We've got twenty-five to do," Laura said with a grin at the two of them. She pulled a needle out of her coveralls and gave the horse a shot before Dottie led it away.

"Want me to move your truck closer?" Mac asked, aiming another stream of tobacco toward the open doors.

"Would you mind?" Laura said. "Buddy's in there, but he knows you."

Mac went out the double doors as Dottie led another horse from its stall. Connie and James came with her. She directed them to hook the horse to the cross-ties.

Connie patted the horse's neck before retreating to where

her mother and Jo stood. James ducked under the cross-ties, hunching his shoulders around his neck, widening his eyes, and baring his teeth in mock fear.

"Aren't they neat? They're so big," Connie said.

"I want a pinch of that snuff," James remarked in a low voice.

"Yech. It'll eat your mouth out," Connie told him.

"Yeah," he said with feigned enthusiasm. "I want to practice spitting."

Jo smiled, listening to them, forgetting momentarily how cold she was.

Dottie heard, too. "It's a filthy, dirty habit, but most of the horsemen do it. I used to dip once in a while. All that spitting gets in the way when you're in the show ring."

James was momentarily silenced until Dottie asked him and Connie to put away the horse while she got another.

After ten horses, Jo was bone cold, bored, and ready to leave, but by then James and Connie were really into helping. Mac had gone off to get grain, leaving his wife to assist, and she enlisted the two teenagers as her assistants.

"Do you think we can get them out of here without an argument," she whispered into Gail's ear.

"Maybe we can come back and get them," Gail murmured.

Jo caught Laura's eye. The vet was sweating. "I'll bring them home if they want to stay."

Her Sebring sported a thin coating of dust. The sun had vanished behind an armada of clouds and bits of snow drifted down to join the few inches on the ground. In the car, Jo turned on the heat and shivered until she felt some warmth.

"I don't know about you, but I thought I was going to freeze to the floor if I stood there any longer," Gail said. "Nice of Laura to bring the kids home."

"Yeah," she agreed, feeling guilty.

"You're seeing her, aren't you?" Gail asked.

Jo's heart jumped painfully. "I've had supper with her a few times."

Gail turned to look at her. "She's why you leaped at the chance of moving out, isn't she?"

Hesitating, she said, "You met her lover. Wendy. Remember?"

"You're not going to double time me, Jo. I'm not Mark."

Opening her mouth to refute the charge, she said lamely, "If that's what you think . . ."

"That's what I think. Just drop me off at home. Connie's home this weekend anyway. I don't want her to know, by the way."

She reached out a hand to stop Gail when she opened her door at the house. "Don't do this."

"When you make a choice, let me know. I've got to rework my life here."

Terrific, she thought, as she put the car in drive. In shock, she drove mindlessly, sightlessly. There was nowhere she wanted to go, except Gail's. She drove to the library where she picked up books and videos.

From there she phoned Kim, got Anna first, who told her all about what was going on in her little world before finally asking, "Want to talk to Ben?"

"Of course," she said, trying to be patient. "Love you, sweetie."

Then Ben was on the line, regaling her with the details of a video movie they'd watched. "Want to talk to Syd?" he asked.

"Why not?" She laughed. After Sydney, though, Kim came on the line.

"If I hadn't walked by, you'd probably never gotten to talk to me. I am the reason you called, aren't I?"

"They brightened my day, which God knows needs it. Gail guessed about Laura and told me to take a hike till I decide who I want in my life."

"That's civilized of her. What did you expect? That she'd let you bed them both?"

"I expected a little sympathy from you."

"Guess who's coming for Christmas dinner, besides you?"

"Mark? Hey, I haven't told you the latest."

"Mark told me what happened at work. Don't go in the bathroom alone. I guess you haven't listened to your messages. There's one from me. Our father and Thomas are coming."

"Really? I haven't said I was coming."

"Where would you go now? Doesn't Laura have a honey of her own?"

"Don't be nasty," Jo snapped.

"Sorry. I am sorry. I don't really know her, but I like Gail."

Maybe she should have stayed with Mark. Gail had been enough temptation for her then. She hadn't thought to stray any further.

She listened to her messages. It was mid-afternoon. The snowflakes had thickened. She turned on the lights, the music, and sat down with a book in her favorite leather chair, the one facing the big bay window, the yard and river beyond. She was drawn into the story.

When she lifted her head next, dusk had fallen. Except for the music, there was no sound. It was as if she were the only person in the complex. She could be, she thought, since it was Saturday night. She sliced some cheese and got out a box of crackers, mixed herself a vodka and tonic, and returned to the chair and her book.

The phone was at her elbow and when it rang, she started. "Jo here."

"Connie here," the girl mimicked.

"Hi, Connie. How was the rest of your time at the stable?"

"Dottie let us brush the horses; she showed us how to clean their feet. That was kind of yucky, but the rest was fun. She said we could help out anytime our moms wanted to bring us out. Clean stalls and stuff. We're going tomorrow afternoon."

"Good. What's up?" she asked, switching ears and gazing out at the lamplit yard.

"That's what I was going to ask you. Mom's in the bedroom crying. Why don't you come over?"

"Does she want me to? Ask her."

The receiver clanged as if it had fallen to the floor. Moments later, Connie returned. "No, she doesn't. What did you do?"

"I don't come on the weekends you're there. Remember?"

"What if I want you here?"

"I can't come if she doesn't want me too. Call me if anything changes."

"But did you have a fight or something?"

"I wouldn't call it a fight. Talk to your mom."

Off the phone, she continued to stare out the window, her book in her lap. Let Gail explain the split-up to her daughter. It was her idea.

Turning off the music, she put in a video and fell asleep in the middle of it.

Sunday afternoon, she puttered around the house, picking things up for the cleaning service that came on Mondays. At four o'clock the phone rang. Connie was on the other end.

"Mom's not home and neither is James' mom. Can you pick us up? We're at the stable."

"Maybe one or the other is on her way."

"They're not. I told Mom James' mom would pick us up and he told his mom my mom would get us. And now they're both gone."

"Did you call your dad?"

"You don't want to come?"

"Of course I do, Connie. I don't want to step on any toes, is all. I'll take you home and drop you off."

She hopped in her car and drove to the stable where she parked and went inside to find Connie and James. The same cold air and sweet, dusty smell of feed greeted her. Several riders sat their horses in the middle of the arena. Connie and James stood at the rail, watching.

"Ready?" she asked with a smile.

Connie held a yellow kitten in her arms. The tiny feline kneaded her arm with its claws. "Think I should take him home for Boo?"

"No."

"I rescued him from the dogs."

She had seen the dogs on Saturday when they rode off with Mac in the back of his truck. "Well, put it somewhere safe and we'll go."

"I'll hide it in the hay," James offered.

The riders of the horses in the center of the ring were taking turns on the rail. She and Connie leaned on the boards and watched them pass by. Jo heard the creak of leather, the breathing of the animals, the thud of their hooves in the sand.

"What did you do today?"

"Cleaned stalls, groomed horses. Dottie says we can ride as soon as our moms give written permission." The girl glowed.

"Would you like to have a horse?"

"That'll never happen. It costs too much money. Ask Mom." Connie's blue eyes met hers and held. "Will you come for dinner?"

"If your mom calls and asks me to dinner, but she won't, and I'm not going inside if she's not there."

James returned, his hands in the pockets of his jacket, a big grin on his face. His dark, lank hair hung over his eyes. Freckles stood out on his nose and cheeks. He was cute.

"Okay, let's go," Jo said.

On the way home, Connie sat in front and chattered to both of them — about the horses, the dogs, the cats — until Jo stopped listening. In the rearview mirror, she watched James stare out the window.

"We're going back next Saturday, aren't we James?"

"If I can get away. Mom might need me."

"Come on, James. Just this next time. Then I can go alone," Connie urged.

"I'll try," he said.

Jo dropped James off at his house a few blocks away from Gail's, then pulled into Connie's driveway and parked under the overhang. She left the engine running.

"Come on in. Mom's home."

Jo shook her head and smiled. She had none of her clothes for tomorrow's work day.

"Just for a minute."

She sighed and gave in. "Just for a minute," she repeated.

Gail met them in the kitchen, her green eyes dark with emotion, her arms crossed. "Thanks for picking her up," she said. "Why didn't you call me, Connie?"

"I did."

"No, you didn't. I was here all afternoon."

"I gotta go upstairs. Be right back," Connie said, scooping up the cat and carrying him with her.

"How are you?" Jo tried out a smile. It slipped off her face.

"Not so good. And you?"

She shrugged. "Lonely. Connie wanted me to come in. I'm sorry. I shouldn't have."

"It's easier if I don't see you," Gail said, "but now do you believe that she likes you?"

"I like her too. It's too bad you two can't get into sync," she said.

"Too bad you can't make up your mind," Gail retorted.

She hesitated, her hand on the knob, waiting for an invitation. "See you."

"Bye."

XXIII

At that moment she decided to continue seeing Connie. She wouldn't go out of her way to do so. Connie would have to make the overtures, but why avoid the kid? It would also be a way to stay in touch with Gail.

The days marched on toward Christmas. Jo filled her free time shopping. She had to get her mother and Stan's gifts in the mail, so they came first. Since they were golfers, she made the rounds of golf shops, looking at clothes and knick knacks. She bought nice playing cards with bridge score pads.

After she finished their shopping, wrapped, and mailed the packages, she bought gifts for everyone else. She consulted Kim about presents for the kids and Brad. Consulting her lists, she marched through stores, mulling over outfits and toys and books. Kim had offered to get something from both of them for their father and Thomas.

Lastly, she looked for something to give Laura, Connie, and Gail. Laura was difficult. She secretly perused her book shelves, her CD collection. In desperation, she bought her a pair of gold earrings with a small horse hanging from each.

Then came Connie. She asked Gail for sizes. Gail asked why. "Don't give her false hope that you're coming back."

"Come on, Gail, it's you who's keeping me away," she shot back.

Gail gave her the information, then added, "Don't buy me anything."

"I'm going to. I may not give it to you right away, though."

"Forget it," Gail said. "I've got to go."

"Where are you going?"

"What's it to you?" Gail asked.

"You're friendly tonight," she said. "I'll let you go gladly."

"My pleasure."

A little later Connie called as she did every few nights. She sounded shy. "Mom's gone out with her friends. Don't tell her I called. Okay?"

"I won't. What's up?" She was in the kitchen, wolfing down leftover pork stew before hitting the mall.

"Where are you going to be Christmas? We're not going to Grandma and Grandpa's because they're going to Florida. My dad and his family are going to be gone too."

"My sister Kim's house. Our father will be there." She wondered if Mark would show up too. The divorce was proceeding smoothly.

"Can you come over here Christmas day?" The girl sounded forlorn.

"Maybe for an hour or two." She had to give Connie her gift. "How's James?"

"He's got a boyfriend. We're still friends, but it's different now. You know? I feel weird around them."

She could guess, of course. "Have you been out at the

stable?" She hadn't seen Connie since the Sunday she gave her a ride home.

The girl's voice brightened. "Yeah. I got to ride the other day. James doesn't really like riding, but I do."

"I'll have to come see you on a horse."

"How about Saturday? You could meet me there."

"I could take you there. How about that?"

"Cool."

Carol had been behaving strangely. Jo attributed her edginess to Csyzka still being on the loose. She walked into the office the next morning and paused at Carol's desk as she did every day and tried to get the woman's gaze to rest on her. Carol was looking over her shoulder as if she expected Csyzka to suddenly appear.

"He's not here, Carol." She put a hand on her shoulder and Carol flinched. "Sorry. Didn't mean to startle you."

"I'm the one who's sorry."

Jo frowned, but then Walter walked in and diverted her attention. He followed Jo into her office.

"No coffee yet." She went over to the shelf under the window behind her desk and flipped the switch on the coffee machine she'd filled at the end of the previous day.

"I can wait." He set his briefcase on the floor and sat down with a sigh. Jerking his head toward the mostly closed door, he said, "She's sure jumpy. Wish they'd find him."

"Then she'll have to testify against him."

"One of us probably will too," he pointed out. "It's nice that she has Mark to lean on. I think she needs the support he gives her. He can tell her what's going to happen when they do catch that piece of slime."

Something akin to an electric shock coursed through Jo. She stared at Walter. No wonder Carol wouldn't meet her eyes.

"I thought you knew," he said, flushing.

"She told me Mark called her at home after the assault, but I thought it was a one time thing."

"I guess he's decided she needs him." Walter cleared his throat and pulled himself up in the chair.

She sat down and said too blithely, "He doesn't have to answer to me anymore."

"Maybe it's just an attorney client relationship," Walter said.

Waving a hand in dismissal, she got up to pour the coffee. "Maybe it is. I'm glad I know." She needed to bring this knowledge into the open. Neither she nor Carol should feel so awkward.

Sipping the coffee, she leaned back in her chair and waited for Walter to speak.

"Your brew is always better than mine. That's why I come in here first thing in the morning." He lowered his voice. "I'm wondering if she should take a little time off from work."

Jo lifted her shoulders. "I don't know. She probably needs to keep busy. Ask her."

"You're a woman. You ask her."

She studied him long enough to make him squirm a little, then nodded. "All right. Send her in when you leave and I will."

Carol moved differently, furtively. She took the chair Walter had vacated and accepted the cup of coffee Jo poured as if in a daze.

Jo walked over and closed the door. Sitting in her chair behind the desk, she smiled at the receptionist. "Walter thought maybe you might like some time off."

Carol panicked. "No. I have to work. I'd go crazy sitting at home."

"Hey, nobody's trying to get rid of you. We need you. You know that. He's thinking of your health."

The woman shifted nervously. "I should get back to my desk."

"Carol, Walter told me about Mark and it's okay. I'm seeing other people. Why shouldn't he?" She struggled with the words, wishing Mark had found someone who didn't work with her, someone she didn't see on a nearly daily basis. Even though she hadn't, she wished he'd waited till the divorce was over.

Carol's big eyes darted in her direction and away. "I like him a lot," she murmured.

"He's a nice man. I like him too." A sour taste flooded her mouth.

"I better go back to work." Carol scuttled out of the room with a fleeting smile.

Saturday she picked Connie up at her house. The girl dashed out the side door as soon as she pulled into the driveway.

"Where's your mom?"

"In bed with a bad cold."

She fought down the urge to leap out of the car and rush to Gail's bedside. "Where'd she pick that up?"

"Two nights a week she goes out with her friends. She stays out too late." Connie settled in the seat. She wore hiking boots, jeans, a sweatshirt and heavy jacket.

Jo had put on jeans, a sweater, tennies, and her down jacket. Beside her were an ear band and mittens. She hadn't forgotten the cold still air of the stable. "Have you met her friends?"

"What do you care anyway? You left." A short-lived outburst.

"Yeah, I guess I did. What do you do when she's gone?"

"Checking up on me again?" Connie shot her a blue-eyed look.

"Are you mad at me or something? I'm just making conversation." Here she'd gone out of her way to take the girl to the stable. Connie was never grateful.

"Sorry," the girl muttered, looking cross. "It's just that nothing's the same anymore. Mom's never home. James has got this boyfriend. You're gone, Dad's gone. No one ever stays in the same place."

Her heart twisted at this brief summary of Connie's life. She sighed. "That must be how it seems."

"You said I could spend the night sometime. Mom's sick. It's my weekend at home. James asked me over, but he and the boyfriend would probably rather be alone."

"You ask your mom," she said, bouncing down the long drive to the stable. "It's okay with me."

A short while later, Jo leaned against the rail in the cold, dusty arena and watched Connie ride. Dressed in a wool lined jeans jacket, her cowboy boots poking out from under worn jeans, Dottie stood next to her and called out to Connie who sat atop a fat palomino gelding:

"Heels down." "Sit deep." "Stay on the rail." "Give him a little rein." "Cluck for a trot." "Touch him with the outside leg and kiss for a canter."

Already Jo was shivering, but Connie looked so intent, so happy, that she made herself show enthusiasm. Smiling when the girl passed, nodding, saying, "Looking good."

"How much are lessons?" she asked Dottie. She had yet to buy Connie anything for Christmas.

"She's earning them by cleaning stalls." Dottie turned bright brown eyes on her. "I like to encourage kids who really want to ride and can't afford to keep a horse or pay for lessons at twenty-five bucks a crack. She might turn into a real horsewoman. She's got good hands."

"What does that mean?"

"She doesn't hang on a horse's mouth."

"I was thinking of giving her lessons for Christmas but . . ."

"I got a pair of chaps that should fit her. She could use 'em. Keeps the cold out and saves wear on the jeans."

While Connie untacked the horse and cleaned its stall, Dottie showed Jo the chaps. They were a light beige color, adorned with silver conchos and fringes, and only slightly shiny on the inside legs.

"If they don't fit, bring 'em back."

Doubtful about giving a second-hand gift, she nevertheless wrote out a check while Dottie stuffed them into a plastic bag.

"I'll hang onto the check till after Christmas," Dottie said, folding it and putting it in her jeans pocket. "I think she'll be thrilled."

Jo hid the chaps in the trunk. When Connie climbed into the car, she smelled of horse.

"Mom doesn't like me in her car after I've been riding. She says I could fool another horse into thinking I'm one too."

"She's got a point," Jo said, hoping the odor wouldn't linger.

"You gonna come in and see her?" Connie asked when they turned onto her block.

"Sure." Her heart fluttered a little in anticipation, but when she followed Connie inside, the house seemed empty. Only Boo greeted them, jumping down from the back of the couch and rubbing against their legs.

"I'll go tell her you're here and get my stuff. Can I take a quick shower?"

"Please do."

"And oh, I have to call James and tell him I'm going to be gone."

Jo stood at the French doors, looking out at the birds on the feeders in the snow covered backyard. She did not hear Gail pad into the room.

"She's spending the night with you?" Gail looked miserable. Her nose red, her face pale, her eyes bloodshot with dark bags under them, her hair flattened on one side. She wore an old bathrobe pulled around her. It did nothing to improve her appearance.

Nodding, she said, "You look terrible. Maybe we should stay here and take care of you."

Gail shook her head. "I'll call if I need someone. I'm not fit to be around. Besides, I'm contagious." She sneezed as if in emphasis. "Did she ask or did you?"

"It doesn't matter. I don't have any other plans. I hear you've been out and about."

"I don't guess it's any of your concern." Gail shrugged. "It's nice, though, her spending the night."

Connie thudded down the stairs and pecked her mother on the cheek. "See ya."

"When are you going to bring her back?" Gail asked, her voice a hoarse croak.

"Tomorrow."

"Want to go Christmas shopping?" she asked the girl when they slammed the doors against the cold wind.

"Yeah. I haven't even started," Connie said, which was no surprise to Jo.

Connie found something for her mother almost immediately. "I've been saving half a year for this," she told Jo proudly as the clerk wrapped the Caphalon all purpose pan. "She's always talking about these kinds of pans."

Gail would be pleased since she loved to cook. It wasn't anything Jo would get for her either. She looked at Connie with renewed respect. "That's a lot of money."

"I know, but I gotta get her something. What are you going to get her?" Connie's blue eyes perused hers.

"I don't know."

"I need to get some things for my other family, too. Can we do some of that?"

Jo looked at the crowds around her. She usually avoided the mall on weekends. They had to do something with the afternoon. "Sure."

On the way home, Jo stopped at Family Video where, after an hour, they agreed on a video. At the Pizza Parlor they ordered a couple of medium size pizzas to go.

Connie remarked after setting the pizzas on the kitchen counter, “This is so cool. Wish we lived here.”

“Yeah, well, neither your mother or I can afford to buy this place.”

They ate the pizzas at the dining room table, washing them down with root beers. “What do you do here alone?” Connie asked.

“Read, listen to music, watch TV, wash clothes, clean. Just what I did at your place.”

“It was a lot more fun when you were there. Mom mopes around the house when she’s home.” Connie shot a sideways look at her, a flash of blue.

She was flattered.

XXIV

Christmas fell on a Monday. Jo spent Christmas Eve with Kim and her family as she would Christmas Day. She brought food for the table and gifts for everyone. Three feet of snow had accumulated through the month.

She phoned Gail in the morning to say she would stop in within the hour. She had promised Connie, who had invited her. The chaps were wrapped as was another James Herriot book. In her purse was a box with a gold band in it. She had bought a sweater and a book to give Gail in its place. The gold band would have to wait until another day.

The little house smelled of pecan rolls and coffee, the Christmas tree and candles. She paused in the kitchen to inhale. Connie danced from one stocking foot to the other in front of her.

"Mom bought me ten riding lessons. I'll clean stalls anyway, though."

"Merry Christmas, Jo," Gail said from the doorway. She'd had her hair cut close to her head. Her green eyes glowed. "Now we can baptise the Caphalon pan Connie gave me."

"You look like one of Santa's elves." Jo stepped forward to give Gail a quick kiss on the cheek before she could back away. "What can I do to help?"

"Have a cup of coffee."

Jo had eaten nothing in hopes of being asked to breakfast. She poured herself a cup and went into the living room to see the tree. The sun leaked through thin clouds, alighting on the cat which was sleeping on the back of the couch. He arched under the hand she ran over his back. She whispered in a twitching ear, "Merry Christmas, Boo."

Setting her gifts under the tree, she sat on the couch and wished she could spend the day here. Connie showed her the gifts she had received from her father and stepmother and half siblings. Then she took a charm bracelet out of a box and held it up to the light.

"From James," Connie said. "He broke up with his boyfriend."

"There'll be others," Jo warned, crossing an ankle over her knee and holding it.

"I know."

"What did you give him?"

"A James Herriot book."

Jo laughed and sniffed the air, smelling the bacon frying in the new pan. Her stomach responded with growls.

"Can I open my presents?" Connie asked, crossing her legs so that the cat could sit in her lap.

"When your mom's here."

They ate first. Homemade coffee cake, bacon, an omelet.

Jo was sure she wouldn't be hungry again till dinner. "You're one wonderful cook, Gail."

"Just your basic fare," Gail demurred. "Who's going to be at Kim's today?"

"I don't know outside of our father and his partner and Kim and her family. How about you?"

Connie shot her mother a quick glance.

"Just a few friends."

Jo tried to keep the smile in place, but she knew it had slipped. "I'll clean up."

"I'll do it. You guys go sit in the living room." Connie jumped to her feet.

She brought her coffee cup to the sofa and let the cat climb into her lap. "You look wonderful, Gail."

Gail pulled her legs up on the recliner. "So do you. I guess being single suits us."

"How single are you?" she asked.

The green eyes flashed. "Don't ask questions. I might answer them."

"Why don't you ever ask?"

"Maybe I don't want to know." Gail smiled. "Connie loves this horse stuff. She'd live at those stables if I let her. I don't know where it came from."

"Weren't you horse crazy as a kid?" Gail shook her head. "I was. Now they just look very big to me."

Connie came in and sat on the floor near the tree. Boo jumped off Jo's lap and curled up in the girl's. "Can we open now?" She started passing around packages.

When Connie pulled the chaps out of the box, Jo flushed. Such a stupid gift, she thought, something that had belonged to someone else. That was not how Connie saw them, though. She let out a little shriek and dumped the cat on the floor as she stood up to try them on.

"They're perfect. Where did you get them?"

"Well, Dottie said she had a pair that might fit you and that you needed some."

"Do I ever! Thanks." She kissed Jo on the cheek and then rubbed the spot with her fingers. "We don't do that, do we?" She tore the wrapping off the book and looked pleased.

"Maybe we should," Jo said, hiding her emotion by opening one of her packages, a box from Gail. In it were a silk blouse and vest.

"Now you have to give Mom a kiss," Connie said, and Jo did. On the cheek.

Gail tried on the sweater that Jo had bought for her and read the blurb on the book, while Jo thought of the band of gold in her purse. She resisted the urge to get it out. It would mean giving up Laura.

Connie again piped up, "Give Jo a kiss, Mom," and watched as Gail planted a kiss to the left of Jo's mouth.

"Open mine, Jo," Connie said, and Jo thought back to last Christmas when Connie cleverly avoided being in the same room with her. Gail's kiss had sent tingles through her.

The small box held a pair of earrings with kingfishers set in a gold circle, delicate and lightweight. She took off the pair she was wearing and put the new ones on. "They're wonderful."

Connie turned her cheek for a kiss. "I know you like birds."

"I do, and I love the earrings. Thank you."

Lastly, she set Boo's wrapped catnip mouse on the floor. They laughed when he tried to tear it open.

Jo wished she were going anywhere else other than Kim's. Mexico on the Pacific would be ideal. But who would she go there with? She wasn't looking forward to polite conversation with relative strangers, like her father and Thomas, nor possibly seeing Mark.

She parked on the curb. There were two strange vehicles in the driveway. Friends often stopped in at Kim and Brad's on Christmas day. Taking the pies and hors d'oeuvres she had fixed at home, she made her way to the front door. She pushed the doorbell with her elbow.

The kids answered, all five of them babbling excitedly. Even Max had lost his cool. He and Ben went out to her car to get the bags she hadn't been able to manage. Lauren took the box of food. Anna carried a pie. Sydney was jumping up and down, extending her arms. Jo picked her up with a laugh and kissed her cheek.

Kim appeared in the hall. Jo knew immediately something was amiss. Her smile froze on her face. "What is it? Is Mark here? Tell me?"

"Brace yourself," Kim whispered into her ear after a kiss on the cheek. "Everybody's here."

"Everybody?" she repeated.

"Well, not yet. Our new found father's on the way and I can't get hold of him to warn him and Thomas."

"Of what?" A terrible angst burned in her throat.

"Mother and Stan showed up on our doorstep an hour ago. They're in the living room right now talking to Mark and Carol."

"Mark and Carol," she repeated angrily. How dare he bring his new woman to her sister's house? She turned toward the door as Max and Ben brought in the bags of gifts. "I'll come back later."

"Oh no you don't," Kim said, taking her by the arm and dragging her into the house. "You're not abandoning me."

She shook herself free. The only way to get through this was to detach herself from her emotions and view it as a spectator at a play.

Her mother stretched out her arms as she and Kim entered the room. "Hello, darling." She and Stan looked out of place with their sun darkened skin.

"What a surprise." She kissed her mother's turned up cheek and hugged Stan who stood behind her mother's chair.

Her eyes darted around the room. A fire flickered on the grate. Carol and Mark stood next to it. She noticed they made a handsome couple, she with her perfect teeth and he with his dark good looks. The tree glowed with color from across the room. Max and Ben knelt on the carpet, adding her gifts to the brightly wrapped boxes underneath it.

"Merry Christmas, Jo," Mark said with a strained smile. "We're just leaving."

Jo nodded at both of them. Her smile didn't quite make it to her face. "Merry Christmas to you both. Hi, Carol."

Carol murmured a reply and dropped her eyes to the carpet. Mark must have dragged her here, Jo thought.

"You all should have come to Florida. I'd forgotten how cold winters are here," her mother piped up.

Brad took the hint and added a small log to the fire. "Glad you stopped by. You're welcome to stay to dinner." He brushed the dirt off his hands and smiled at Mark and Carol.

"We've got to go," Carol said quickly, "but thank you. You've been so kind."

Kim and Brad ushered them to the front door. Jo wondered whether Carol played bridge, whether they would resume their foursomes without her.

When they were gone, she followed Kim to the kitchen where her sister was opening another bottle of champagne. They had started welcoming Christmas with a toast years ago. She grabbed the smoking bottle and poured herself a glass. "Does Mother know who's coming to dinner?" she asked, downing the bubbly.

"I don't know how to tell her. I don't want a scene in front of the kids." Kim said, emptying her glass.

Brad came in to tell them, "Your father just pulled into the driveway, I think."

"Would you show him in?" Kim said, her eyes pleading with her husband.

Ushering them out of the warm kitchen, Brad steered

them toward the front door as the bell rang. The kids rushed past them in a flock, getting there before they did and flinging it open.

Arms heaped with packages, the two men filled the doorway. Their father bent his long frame to get a good look at the kids and greeted each of them with a small wrapped gift and a few words. When he straightened, he smiled broadly as did Thomas. He shook hands with Brad and hugged his daughters, his deep voice filling the hallway so that Jo and Kim shot covert looks toward the living room.

Brad held back with the two men, Jo hoped, to warn them. But nobody had told their mother. She appeared in the hall with Stan behind her, a look of horrified amazement etched on her face.

She supported herself with a hand on the wall. "What? Why?"

Kim tried to explain. "We didn't know you were coming, Mother."

"How often have I come to visit?" Their mother's voice shook with indignation.

"Now Ginger," Stan said, taking his wife's elbow.

She shook him off. "Don't 'Now Ginger' me. What's he doing here? Have you been seeing him all along?"

Their backs against the wall, the kids slid past the adults and disappeared without a sound.

Jo had seen the shocked look on her father's face at seeing his ex-wife. She felt trapped between them, buffeted by her mother's outrage.

"We'll just leave the gifts and go," her father said, looking ready to flee.

"Oh sure, and make me look like the villain," her mother snapped.

"Well, what do you want, Ginger?" he asked.

Brad took a few of the packages out of his and Thomas' arms and slipped along the wall to the living room. Now there were just herself and Kim standing between the two older couples.

Kim piped, “Come on in. Let’s sort this out in the living room over some bubbly.”

Their mother relented. Retreating on Stan’s arm to the chair she had vacated, she sat rigid wearing an aggrieved look.

Brad poured the champagne and Kim distributed the glasses. Lifting her glass, Kim said, “To family,” and drank deeply. “You go next, Brad.”

“Boy, oh boy,” he said with a wry smile. Thomas guffawed, then looked sheepish.

“Jo?” Kim continued.

They did this every holiday, toasting each other with a few words. “Forgive us our expectations,” she said.

“Hmmp,” her mother said, then surprisingly lifted her glass. “To bygones, but I still think you’re a bad influence.”

A smile twisted Joe’s face. “To the spirit of the day.”

Brad poured more champagne all around.

“To a little peace,” Stan said.

Kim gave a slightly hysterical laugh.

“To goodwill,” Thomas added with a contagious grin.

Jo felt the weight of worry lift a little. She glanced at Kim and exaggeratedly wiped her brow.

“I don’t appreciate that, Jo,” her mother said sharply. “I’m doing my best.”

There was a hint of drawl that made Jo smile. “Sorry, Mother.”

“Come on, Jo, let’s get the hors d’oeuvres underway.” Kim took hold of her arm.

Jo didn’t need any urging. She willingly followed Kim to the kitchen.

Somehow they got through the day. At times, humor took over and Thomas was unable to stem his laughter. Her parents actually talked to each other. Once her mother laughed at something her father said.

“You always were funny,” her mother remarked.

“Funny in more than one way,” Joe shot back.

When her father and Thomas shifted toward the front door, saying good-byes to everyone, Kim and Jo and Brad went outside into the cold night with them.

“Thanks again,” Thomas said. “It was an unforgettable experience.”

They laughed, expelling the tension of the day in cloudy breaths.

“Next time we’ll make sure the coast is clear.”

“Next time we’ll give you the cell phone number,” Joe said, handing them each a business card. “I wouldn’t have missed it, though. We’ll talk about this day till the end of ours. Ginger has mellowed.”

“That’s mellow?” Thomas said.

“She was a terror. Sorry I left you two alone with her. I wasn’t brave or sure enough to buck her.” Their father hugged her and Kim, shook hands with Brad again.

Then he and Thomas were gone, their tail lights flickering as they paused at the crossroad.

XXV

Stan and her mother flew home on the third day. Kim took them to the airport, then called Jo at work.

"They were so glad to leave. Always cold even though we turned the heat up, trapped inside with the kids making them play nonstop games. I felt for them. Stan was a treasure. He never complained. Played Monopoly with Lauren and Max till he must have wanted to scream. And Mother wasn't too bad either. She fell for Sydney, sticky hands and all, and was patient with Ben and Anna's constant questions. I doubt if they'll be back anytime soon, but they asked us to visit and I think they meant it. We'll descend on them like the proverbial pack of locusts."

Jo had dropped in the previous night to say good-bye and

stayed for a couple of hours. Her mother had wrung a promise from her to visit within the the next three months. Now she said to Kim, "Thanks for being so long suffering."

"I was, wasn't I? I'm rather proud of myself. Thanks for not walking out Christmas day."

Jo was still fuming over Mark's gall, coming with Carol to Kim's when he knew she would be there. Carol was holed up in her apartment. Csyzka had been apprehended Christmas day at his parents' home. He was now sitting in jail, awaiting trial, unable to come up with bail.

Walter had hired one of their temporary clients to fill in for Carol. Jo realized she'd be happy if the temp worker replaced Carol. It wasn't Mark's fault she'd left, she kept telling herself. She didn't want him to be lonely, but did he have to date someone she worked with?

She left a little late, walking out to her car with Walter. Tucking her head into her coat against a cold wind, she picked up speed.

Unlocking his car, he slid behind the wheel and waited till her engine kicked in before waving and driving away.

There was no need to go to the condo. Gail never called anymore during the week.

Parking outside Laura's barn, she ran toward the back door and unlocked it before Laura could open it. Too cold to wait. Wiping her feet, she went up the steps to the kitchen, hoping to smell food. She had no wish to go out in the cold yet again tonight.

"Terrible out there," she said when Laura met her at the door between the kitchen and dining room. She had changed into sweats which probably meant they would stay in.

"I've got some Chinese carry-out in the fridge."

"Oh, good," she said. In her pocket was the small wrapped box with the gold horse earrings.

Laura poured two glasses of wine and handed her one. "How was your Christmas?"

Remembering, Jo laughed. "You won't believe it. I didn't." Shedding her coat, she changed into jeans.

"I have something for you," Laura said, handing her a package. "Let's sit down for a few minutes and unwind. I spent the last part of the afternoon in a cold barn stitching up a horse's leg."

"How dreadful." She'd fished the box out of her pocket. "I have a little something for you too."

"You first," Laura said with a smile.

Later, while eating the Chinese fare, Laura said, "I'm moving to Florida. Want to come?"

Disbelieving, she said, "What?"

Laura put her fork down and picked up her wine glass. "My veterinary friend in Florida asked me to join her in the business. It's too good to turn down. Besides, I want to end this relationship with Wendy, and that's the only way to do it. Would you come with me?"

"When did this happen?" she asked in dismay.

"Christmas Day. What do you say? There are temp agencies down there and personnel departments."

She looked away from the sincerity in Laura's eyes and said, "I can't."

"Will you think about it?"

"Sure, but this is where I grew up. This is where I belong."

Laura smiled crookedly. "I think I knew you were more attached to Gail than I was to Wendy."

"That's not it." Was it? What about her sister and her nieces and nephews? And what about her mother? God forbid she should live close by. "I know it sounds silly, but I feel rooted here. I always feel displaced when I'm elsewhere very long."

"You can visit, though." Laura smiled.

"You'll find someone else there. When are you going?" A huge ache gathered in her chest. She'd left Mark and Gail. Now Laura was leaving her. Serves me right, she thought.

"As soon as I can tie things together at this end. Sell the house, box my things, give the clinic time to hire someone else. It might be a month, maybe two even." Laura leaned on her arms and gazed into Jo's eyes till Jo looked away.

She felt she'd played the odds and lost. Knowing she was tripped up by her own careless actions, she wondered if she'd cared about anyone but herself when she left Mark and then Gail.

The evening could not be salvaged, not even in bed, where she fought the pain in the back of her throat that was choking her. In the morning, they parted with promises to call each other. But Jo was already putting distance between them.

Jo phoned Gail to ask about her plans for New Year's Eve. "Are we going to bring in the new year together?"

"I already have plans, Jo. You're welcome to come with us. Dinner out and a play."

"No. No thanks. Can I see you New Year's Day?"

"Sure. Why don't you drop over? Connie has been after me to call you."

"Why haven't you?" she asked.

"I just hadn't gotten around to it."

"What time?"

"Around eleven. For brunch."

She hung up, annoyed. Maybe she needed to renew a few old friendships. Right now, she had no heart for it.

Instead, she picked up videos and a bottle of champagne to bring in the new year. Then Laura called.

"Let's go cross country skiing," Laura suggested.

Fuck brunch. "Up north." She wanted to get away.

That was how they happened to be driving on US 51, the wind buffeting Laura's truck on New Year's Eve morning. Jo had called and told Connie she would be out of town and unable to come over for brunch.

"What are you doing on New Year's Eve?" she'd asked.

"James is having a party." The girl had sounded excited. "A sleepover."

"Your mom's going to let you stay at his place all night?" she'd asked, surprised.

"James isn't just any boy, you know," Connie had said patiently. "Besides, one of my girlfriends will be there. Nina. She doesn't have a boyfriend either."

"I see," she said.

"When are you coming over again?" the girl asked.

"I don't know, Connie, but if you need a ride to the stable anytime, let me know."

Now she watched the snow whip horizontally across the highway close to the ground. It would be cold on the trails, but she always warmed up once she got going.

In Minocqua they checked into the Best Western on the lake, then headed out to Winter Park. Carrying their cross country equipment to the lodge, they leaned the skis and poles against the racks and went inside to put on their boots. Jo wondered how many layers of clothing would be just right and were they crazy to go out into wind chills that were below zero.

Pulling her shell over her head, donning a knitted earband and neckpiece and grabbing mittens, she followed Laura out the door into the wind. They stepped into their skis and poled off, picking up a rhythm. Skate skiers passed them as if they were standing still, even the kids. Her eyes watered and she shivered in the open field.

Once in the woods, though, starting up a steep slope, she began to heat up. The trails were wide, tracks on each side for diagonal skiers such as they, leaving the space in-between for the skate skiers.

After four hours of nonstop sliding, gliding, duck walking up the steeper inclines and whizzing or snow plowing down the long declines, she used her poles to speed her way to the lodge. On her mind now was the hot tub where she would soak her tired legs and shoulders. She'd had one bad fall, hitting her back and head when losing control on a downhill turn. Laura had fallen on the same hill.

"You won't be able to do this on weekends," she pointed out as they put their skis in the rack and went inside for a moment.

The wind blew less fiercely, the sun hung low and yellow. The temperature had dipped. Inside, steam rose from wet clothes and puddles of melted snow on the floor.

"I never got to ski much anyway. I worked too many weekends." Laura sat on a bench to unlace her boots.

Jo did the same. "I'll miss you."

"You don't have to. You can come with me."

"Oh sure. I don't have a job waiting for me." She felt gravity taking her down. "Are you ready?"

After the hot tub, they dressed and crossed the street to eat. The table on the porch gave them a view of the frozen lake across which snowmobiles zipped. A combo played in a corner of the bar.

The place began filling up with revelers, who climbed the steps to the main floor.

Jo sipped her wine and thought about the changes the year had wrought. She was fast sinking into a funk that threatened to ruin the evening. She said brightly, "Think we'll make it till midnight?"

Laura smiled a little. "I seldom do. How do you like to spend New Year's Eve."

"In good company."

They lingered over the remains of their meal, enjoying the live music, until Jo found herself falling asleep. Laura laughed when her chin fell on her chest.

"Come on, woman. Time to go."

The frigid air revived her. They paused in the parking lot to look at the stars. A jet passed high overhead, trailing a plume like a shooting star.

In the warm motel room, Jo fell fast asleep with the television and lights on. She wakened to boots clumping up and down the outside stairs, voices calling back and forth, snowmobiles sawing the quiet into pieces, and the gong falling in Times Square on TV.

"Happy New Year." Laura lay next to her, hands behind her head, her face illumined by the television and the cracks of light peeking inside between blinds and window frames.

"Is it midnight?" she asked.

"In New York it is."

Laura's feather light fingers sent goose bumps chasing each other across her skin. "I'll miss making love to you."

"Me too," she said.

"You will visit me, won't you?"

"Once or twice a year. Will you come back?" She moaned a little as Laura's hand moved in slow motion over her breasts.

"Where would I stay? With you and Gail?"

Breathing deeply as the hand slipped beneath her undershirt, she said, "Don't you have family?"

"Not here." Now the hand moved downward, and Jo lifted her hips in response.

"Where?" Jo asked, concentrating only on the fingers that lifted the elastic of her panties and slid inside.

"They're scattered. My friends are my family." Laura's teeth gently nipped the fleshy part of Jo's ear.

Jo turned her head, pulling her ear away, and took Laura's lower lip between her teeth. "You are a sexy woman," she whispered, moving to embrace her.

The next morning, stiff from the day before, they set out for the American Legion State Forest after breakfast.

The wind bit into any exposed skin. These trails were narrower with some very steep hills. No other vehicles were parked in the lot. They set off at a brisk speed, determined to take advantage of being there.

At the halfway point, someone had started a fire in the pit in front of the shelter. Chickadees flitted back and forth from the platform feeder to the nearby trees, filling the silence with their cheerful chatter.

It was too cold to pause for long. The snow conditions were very fast under their skis. They sped toward the parking lot, taking a short expert trail on the way, one with lots of curves, lots of hills that led past a small lake. Fifteen minutes from start to finish, it left Jo breathless.

"Shall we call it a day?" Laura asked.

Jo glanced at her watch and thought of Gail's little house, the table set with good food. She shivered as the wind found its way through her clothes. "I'm ready to go."

XXVI

The answering machine blinked insistently, demanding her attention. She turned on lights before pushing the button and hearing Kim wish her a happy new year. Then Connie's young voice sobbed into the quiet room that Boo Boo had escaped and no one could find him, would she help look.

It was late afternoon on New Year's day. Jo had no wish to go out into the cold again, but she picked up the receiver and punched in Gail's number.

"Did you find the cat?" she asked when Gail answered.

"I thought you were coming over for brunch."

"I told Connie I couldn't make it. I went skiing." Then she was annoyed with herself for telling Gail where she'd been. Gail never shared her outings.

"No, we haven't found the cat. Connie's outside now looking."

"She called asking if I'd help look."

"When he gets cold enough, don't you think he'll show up?"

"I don't know. I'm coming over anyway. Tell Connie."

Reluctantly, she got into the Sebring and made the trek to Gail's. Instead of dying down, the wind had increased. As day turned into night, the temperature dropped. She worried about the cat who was used to warm rooms.

The headlights illuminated Connie as she turned the car into Gail's driveway. Parking, she got out of the vehicle and went to the girl. "No luck, huh?"

Tears had frozen on the girls red face. "He'll freeze to death."

Putting a hand on Connie's shoulder, she said, "Did you look under the porch?"

"Yeah. He's not there."

"He'll find shelter. Think of the barn cats. They're out in all kinds of weather."

"That's what Mom said. She just doesn't want to be outside anymore." Connie wiped her nose with the back of her mitten.

Who would choose to be out in this incredible cold? "Come on. Let's go inside."

The girl shook her head and began calling again. "I can't."

"All right. You hang around the house. I'll head on down the street." She didn't expect to find the cat, but she had to make a show of looking.

Feet and face and hands freezing, she called as she walked. Her heart jerked painfully when she saw the small shape in the street and slowly headed toward it. Under the streetlight, the mangled animal lay stretched out, exposed, its bloodied mouth open in a grimace. The color of the coat was wrong, though, she saw with relief.

Hearing her name on the crisp air, she straightened.

Connie was running toward her, and she quickly deserted the corpse. "Stay there. I'm coming."

"Mom caught him by the bird feeders out back." The girl's steps slowed. "What's that in the street?"

"Never mind," she said, but Connie went out to examine the furry remains.

Hand covering her mouth, she said, "It looks like James' cat. We have to get him off the road."

"I'll get the shovel," she said without hesitation. Grabbing the snow shovel by the side door, she hurried to where Connie stood over the cat.

They scooped the small frozen body off the pavement. "I'll take him home. You run ahead and get a box."

Head bare, Gail was placing an old towel in the cardboard boot box Connie had retrieved from the garage. "Put him in here," she said. Jo shook the cat off the shovel into the box.

"I'll call James," Connie said in a shaky voice.

"Let's put him in the back hall for now." Gail looked tired as if she'd been up most of the night.

Jo was exhausted but she picked up the box, surprised at the weight of the cat, and carried it inside. Boo yowled from his kennel in the kitchen.

Sitting on the inside top step, she stared down at the dead animal. There was something obscene about death, she thought, how it stripped away the defenses and left the victim bared for all to see.

"Come on in, Jo. I've got a pot of decaf going." Gail broke through her thoughts.

Jo sighed wearily and tripped over the step into the kitchen as Connie got off the phone. "How is James?"

"Bawling," Connie said. "He and his mom are coming to get Piebald."

"Poor Piebald," Gail murmured and flicked a look at Jo. "Lucky Boo."

"I'm going to give him Boo," Connie announced.

"You are not," Jo said sharply. "I have a monetary stake

in that cat. James shouldn't have let Piebald run loose. Cats don't belong outside."

A few minutes later a stricken James and his mother loaded the dead feline in the trunk of their car. Unable to speak, James let his mother do the talking. "Thanks for getting him off the street."

"Where are you going to bury him?" Connie sobbed, her blue eyes running with tears.

"We'll have to put him in the deep freeze in the garage till we can dig a hole, honey," James' mother said.

"Sit down, Jo," Gail said when the car pulled out of the driveway in a veil of exhaust.

Connie knelt and released Boo from the kennel. Tail high, the cat stalked off. Jo laughed, drawing startled looks from Connie and Gail.

"He's so ungrateful," she said. "How'd he get loose anyway?"

"He snuck out when people were going in and out."

"We've got leftovers from brunch. You're welcome to help us finish them off," Gail said, taking covered dishes out of the fridge.

She stayed. There was nothing to eat at the condo but dried up pieces of pizza. Connie carried the conversation, which limped along without her.

"James loved Pie. I wouldn't give Boo away. I was just feeling bad for James. You know? I mean it seems unfair for one to die and the other to live."

Gail looked at her daughter. "That's life. It's not fair."

Jo swallowed and said, "Nothing's fair. It just is."

"Do you believe that?" Gail asked.

"Isn't that what you just said in so many words?" Jo countered.

"Hey, you guys are having a conversation," Connie put in.

"No, we're not," Gail discounted. "This is stupid."

Jo was too tired to disagree and left after the coffee and leftovers were gone.

* * * * *

At the condo, Jo turned up the heat and climbed into the whirlpool bathtub. She thought she'd never get warm again. Phoning Kim while the steam rose around her, she wished her sister a happy new year too, before leaning her head against the ceramic tile and saying, "Laura's moving to Florida, and she wants me to go with her."

"You could see more of Mother."

Jo laughed. "I'm not going. I might visit, though."

"So it's over," Kim pointed out.

"I guess so." She told Kim about finding James' dead cat while searching for Boo.

"Now's your chance to make things right with Gail."

"What do you hear from Mark?"

"He and Carol were at our New Year's Eve party, the one you begged out of. Don't be mad at them, Jo."

She closed her eyes. "I'm not, but do you and Brad have to treat the two of them like she's me all over again? You're my family. Let them spend time with their families."

"She can never take your place. You know that. But Brad likes Mark. They have a lot in common."

"I don't want to talk about them right now."

"She's working in his office starting tomorrow. You won't have to see her every day anyway."

She found out the next day that Carol had resigned. Walter replaced her with two of their temp workers.

The next few weeks Jo lived in a sort of limbo, not allowing herself to dwell on Laura's move. One week night when she and Laura had allowed a sudden rush of passion to get in the way of filling boxes, Jo thought maybe she would follow her to Florida. That notion faded afterwards as she cooled off.

The mental distancing Jo had started the day Laura told

her she was moving had widened. Now she thought of Laura more as a friend than a lover. Yet Gail was still hobnobbing with her other friends, keeping her distance. Jo felt as if she were on her own, increasingly cut off from both of them. Laura would draw her close with sex or conversation, then let her snap away by talking about her future plans. Gail simply ignored her, except when Jo took Connie home from the stable or picked her up.

At the end of the month Laura loaded a U-Haul with her furniture and belongings, hooked her truck to the tow bar, and drove to Florida. The house was sold, the new owners' ready to move in.

Jo followed her to the first crossroads where she turned off toward the stable to meet Connie. She was glad she'd agreed to give the girl a ride home. Feeling alone and despairing, swallowing and blinking back tears, she parked in front of the long white building and went inside.

Connie was riding the palomino in the indoor arena along with three other girls on their horses. She waved and cantered over to where Jo stood at the railing. "Almost ready. Mom wants you to come to dinner."

Good, she thought. She didn't to be alone. Burying her gloved hands in her jacket, she smiled as Dottie joined her. "Connie's doing really well. I'm going to take her to some of the open shows come spring."

"Does she know?" she asked.

"I told her if she keeps working hard that's what we'll do."

"Thanks, Dottie," she said as if Connie were her daughter. "I'm happy for her."

"She deserves it."

On the way home, Connie talked horses.

"How's James doing? Did he get another cat?" Jo asked to change the subject.

"Huh? Oh yeah. He got a kitten and it's so naughty."

"Doesn't he go to the stable with you anymore?"

"Sometimes he and my friend Nina both go, but not today. He and I are going over to Nina's when I get home."

"Did your mom really tell you to ask me to dinner? Be honest. I'm not going to barge in on her." She looked at the girl.

"She tried to call you. You weren't home."

She felt grubby, having spent the morning hours helping Laura clean the house and finish loading the U-Haul. "I should go home and shower first."

"You can shower at our house," Connie said with a dimpled smile.

"Things are different, Connie. You know that."

"Yeah, well, you're both a couple of stupes," the girl said.

"You are such a nervy kid. You know that?"

"You know what James said?"

"How would I?" Jo asked.

"He said you can say anything as long as it's not boring. Nobody likes a bore."

"Nobody likes a smart alec either," Jo said, but laughed.

Gail opened the side door and urged them inside. "Phew. You better go shower, kiddo."

"I don't smell much better," Jo said.

An open bottle of red wine stood on the counter. "You smell better than she does. You don't rub up against the horses anyway. Will you stay for dinner?"

Jo had forgotten how Gail's smile warmed her. It had been a long time since she'd seen that welcoming grin. "Sure."

Pouring them each a glass, Gail lifted hers to her lips. "Connie's spending the night at Nina's."

"Is she?" she said. Gail's eyes bore into her until she felt her heart knocking at her ribs. "What's going on?"

Gail shrugged and busied herself at the stove. The smell of onion and garlic sizzling in a little cooking oil set Jo's stomach churning. "Hungry?" Gail asked, setting out a bowl of avocado dip and a basket of chips. "Take the edge off."

Unzipping her purse on the floor next to her, Jo felt around inside it for the box. It lay at the very bottom, among the coins and little pieces of lint. She began to dip the chips.

Connie came to say good-bye, her hair hanging in wet strands. Gail gave her daughter a kiss and told her to put on a hat and not to stay up all night.

"Thanks for the ride," Connie said to Jo.

"Anytime, kiddo," Jo said. "Have a good time."

When the door closed behind Connie, Gail remarked, "I wish she cared more about how she looks. She never tries to do anything with her hair."

"She dyed it once," Jo said, dipping another chip. "This is good stuff."

Gail turned and grasped the back of the chair. "How are you, Jo?"

Jo jumped, sure that Gail was referring to Laura's move. "Good, fine," she said quickly. "How are you?"

Sighing, Gail said, "Well, I miss you."

"Oh, we're telling the truth," she said with a wry smile. "In that case, substitute lonely and lost for good and fine."

Gail studied her, a small frown creasing the space between her eyes. She took her lower lip between her teeth as if to bite back words.

Jo knew the time had come. It was finally clear. She pulled the box out of her purse, got up, and walked around the table. A smile trembled on her lips. "This is for you. I've had it since before Christmas, waiting for the right moment. I think it's now."

Gail looked at the little box wrapped in Christmas paper.

"Open it," Jo urged.

Inside, the gold band shone as brightly as it had the day she bought it. Her eyes rested on Gail's face.

"What does this mean?" Gail asked.

Jo took the band out of the box. "Give me your hand." She slid the band on the left ring finger and licked her lips. "It means I love you."

"You would catch me like this," Gail said in a hoarse voice. "I don't have a ring for you. I didn't expect this. I had no idea." She lifted her gaze.

"You like it?" Jo smiled with more assurance.

"I love it. I love you too. I never stopped, but I have nothing to give you right now."

"Oh yes you do." She smiled.

Cold air rushed into the room as the door swung open. Connie stood in the opening, glancing from one to the other. "You two are so gross," she said, but with a wide grin. "Go ahead and kiss, you perverts. Don't let me stop you." Grabbing her forgotten backpack off the hook on the wall near the door, she slammed out the door.

Jo looked at Gail, and they broke into laughter. Gail gasped between whoops, "I told you she likes you."

"Come here, and I'll show you what a pervert I am." Jo said, closing the distance between them.

Gail took the remaining step. "Promises, promises."

About the Author

Jackie Calhoun's books include *Lifestyles, Second Chance, Sticks and Stones, Friends and Lovers, Triple Exposure, Changes, For Love or Money, Seasons of the Heart, By Reservation Only, Birds of a Feather, Off Season,* and *Tamarack Creek*. Calhoun lives with her partner in Northeast Wisconsin.

CALM BEFORE THE STORM by Peggy J. Herring.
pp. Colonel Robicheaux retires from the military and
comes out of the closet. ISBN

OFF SEASON by Jackie Calhoun. 208 pp. Pam thre
Jenny and Rita's fledgling relationship. ISBN

WHEN EVIL CHANGES FACE: A Motor City Thri
by Therese Szymanski. 240 pp. Brett Higgins is ba
another heart-pounding thriller. ISBN

BOLD COAST LOVE by Diana Tremain Braund.
Jackie Claymont fights for her reputation and the
love the woman she chooses. ISB

THE WILD ONE by Lyn Denison. 176 pp. Rachel
expected that Quinn's wild yearnings would chan
life forever. IS

SWEET FIRE by Saxon Bennett. 224 pp. Welcon
Heroy — the town with the most lesbians per ca
any other place on the planet! IS

Publications from

BELLA BOOKS, INC.

the best in contemporary lesbian fiction

P.O. Box 201007 Ferndale, MI 48220
Phone: 800-729-4992
www.bellabooks.com

OUTSIDE THE FLOCK by Jackie Calhoun. 224 pp. Jo embraces her new love and life. ISBN 1-931513-13-9 $12.95

LEGACY OF LOVE by Marianne K. Martin. 224 pp. Read the whole Sage Bristo story. ISBN 1-931513-15-5 $12.95

STREET RULES: A Detective Franco Mystery by Baxter Clare. 304 pp. Gritty, fast-paced mystery with compelling Detective L.A. Franco ISBN 1-931513-14-7 $12.95

RECOGNITION FACTOR: 4th Denise Cleever Thriller by Claire McNab. 176 pp. Denise Cleever tracks a notorious terrorist to America. ISBN 1-931513-24-4 $12.95

NORA AND LIZ by Nancy Garden. 296 pp. Lesbian romance by the author of *Annie On My Mind.* ISBN 1931513-20-1 $12.95

MIDAS TOUCH by Frankie J. Jones. 208 pp. Sandra had everything but love. ISBN 1-931513-21-X $12.95

BEYOND ALL REASON by Peggy J. Herring. 240 pp. A romance hotter than Texas. ISBN 1-9513-25-2 $12.95

ACCIDENTAL MURDER: 14th Detective Inspector Carol Ashton Mystery by Claire McNab. 208 pp.Carol Ashton tracks an elusive killer. ISBN 1-931513-16-3 $12.95

SEEDS OF FIRE:Tunnel of Light Trilogy, Book 2 by Karin Kallmaker writing as Laura Adams. 274 pp. Intriguing sequel to *Sleight of Hand.* ISBN 1-931513-19-8 $12.95

DRIFTING AT THE BOTTOM OF THE WORLD by Auden Bailey. 288 pp. Beautifully written first novel set in Antarctica. ISBN 1-931513-17-1 $12.95

CLOUDS OF WAR by Diana Rivers. 288 pp. Women unite to defend Zelindar! ISBN 1-931513-12-0 $12.95

OUTSIDE THE FLOCK by Jackie Calhoun. 220 pp. Searching for love, Jo finds temptation. ISBN 1-931513-13-9 $12.95

WHEN GOOD GIRLS GO BAD: A Motor City Thriller by Therese Szymanski. 230 pp. Brett, Randi, and Allie join forces to stop a serial killer. ISBN 1-931513-11-2 $12.95

DEATHS OF JOCASTA: 2nd Micky Night Mystery by J.M. Redmann. 408 pp. Sexy and intriguing Lambda Literary Award nominated mystery. ISBN 1-931513-10-4 $12.95